Graves & Griggs
A Very Bloody Christmas

KATELYN TAYLOR

Playlist

You've Created a Monster by Bohnes
It's Beginning to Look a Lot Like Christmas by Michael Bublé
Lips of a Witch by Austin Giorgio
Same Damn Time by Future
Butterfly by Crazy Town
A GOOD DAY TO DI3 by Arankai
You're a Mean One, Mr. Grinch by Thurl Ravenscroft
LET THE WORLD BURN by Chris Grey
Puppet by Stain The Canvas
Have Yourself a Merry Little Christmas by Frank Sinatra

Copyright

Published by Katelyn Taylor

Cover by Booklovedesigns

Edited by Ten Thousand | Editing + Book Design

Proofreading by Judy's Proofreading

Graves & Griggs is a work of fiction.

Names, characters, incidents, and places are used fictitiously. Any resemblance to real people or events is coincidental.

Graves & Griggs: A very bloody Christmas

Copyright © 2025 by Katelyn Taylor

All rights reserved.

Trigger Warning

Please carefully consider the following triggers included in this story. As you may have predicted, this book is full of dark, explicit and grotesque scenes that should not be taken lightly. These triggers include but are not limited to:

knife play, bloody play, sharing, explicit sexual scenes, explicit violence, graphic torture, mercenary work, shooting in a public space (no civilians), mention of cannibalism, home invasion, DDLG play, breeding, DP, anal, exhibition/voyeurism, holiday torture, body parts used as a puppet, postpartum depression, mental illness, pregnancy and difficult labor mentioned.

Dedication

To the lovers of Graves and Gallows Hill who are craving a bloody good festive book!

Prologue
Zayden

I'm listening to the doc go on and on about preparing my angel for labor. She's thirty-seven weeks, which is pretty much a miracle for twins—our own mom made it to thirty-five before her water popped. Then again, wouldn't have put it past her to induce herself so she could go get her fix. Like her being pregnant stopped that anyways. Junkie bitch.

Dominic is listening with rapt attention while I'm sitting on the exam table, my angel tucked between my legs. The doc tried to get me off the exam table, just like she does every appointment. You'd think she'd have given up by this point. Where my angel goes, I go. Simple as that. She doesn't even fight it anymore, just gives me a patient smile while Dominic shakes his head. It's a nice little dynamic we have set up.

My fingers twist her wedding rings around on her hand as the doc continues. I'll still never get over the fact that this perfect fucking angel married *me*. Technically, me and my brother, but if you ask me, she just agreed to marry him because she felt bad. We all know I'm her favorite.

Not only did she marry me, though—us—but now she's giving us the most precious thing in the world. A family. Two sons.

"Do you have any questions?" the doc asks, looking at my angel briefly before her eyes find Dominic, who's looking at his phone, no doubt at the mile-long list he's compiled since the last appointment. He's been really on top of all the medical stuff during her pregnancy, and I've been there to rub her back and eat her pussy anytime she's uncomfortable. It's a balance.

My phone rings in my pocket, and irritation rises inside me as I pull it out and glance at the screen. An unknown number, no surprise there. No doubt it's a job. We still take on jobs here and there, but not like we used to. We don't feel the need—well, Dominic and my angel don't. I get a little stabby from time to time and will pick up something last minute for a little release. It's like therapy for me. I know what you're thinking: maybe I should try actual therapy. C'mon, though—killing worthless fucks who have it coming is so much more fun.

I tap Blake's thigh, signaling that I'm going to take the call, and she scooches to the side. I slide off the table, pressing a kiss to her head before I step out of the room and answer.

"What?" I snap into the phone.

A voice I haven't heard in a while echoes through the phone.

"Not very good manners, Graves. Is that how everyone on the West Coast begins new conversations?" Christopher Putnam asks.

I roll my eyes in annoyance, not the least bit impressed by this slimy prick.

He runs a secret society out in Salem, Massachusetts, called the Brethren. Though, if you ask me, they operate pretty loud for being a "secret." Maybe the secret part is what their motives truly are. I've heard rumors that they're descended from witches or the people who killed the witches in the Salem witch trials. Something like that. If you ask Putnam, I'd say he more closely aligns himself to Christ, though. The fucking asshat thinks he walks on water or some shit. We haven't gotten a call from him in years, mainly because they have in-house men that take care of their needs. So why the fuck is he bothering me?

"What do you want, Putnam?" I sigh heavily.

A raspy chuckle echoes through the phone, and I can practically see his smile curling his face up as he continues.

"I have a job that I would love your hands on. We're doing some remodeling and could use a man with your skills."

"Yeah? How big is the remodel?" I ask as I walk down the hall.

"Not too bad. One room, easily manageable, as long as our timing lines up."

The Brethren is calling me all the way out to the East Coast for one kill? Very unlike them. Consider my interest officially piqued.

"And what does the job pay?" I ask, strolling over to the front desk where a jar of lollipops sits out.

I grab a cherry one for my angel, her favorite, before I grab one for myself and pop it into my mouth. I close my eyes; I can already taste the cherry flavor on her lips.

"Triple our standard rate," he says, catching me off guard.

The rate Dom and I have in place with the Brethren is $250,000. Whoever this target is, Putnam is willing to spend three-quarters of a million dollars to make them disappear?

"When?" I ask.

"You have three days."

I don't love the idea of leaving town with Blake so close to her due date. I'll call my contact at the airport, get on a private jet. I can leave tonight and be back by breakfast.

"I'll be there tonight. Send me the details."

"Already sent," he says before the line goes dead.

I pull my phone away from my ear, looking down at the incoming text message.

An address and a coded name.

Griggs.

Damn, that's a shame. I actually liked that kid. He reminds me of a version of myself. He's not nearly on my level, but he's in his early twenties—he's got time. According to this text, though, not much time at all. I knew his parents for years; we always ran into each other on jobs. Maxim and Putnam seemed to always have similar enemies. I've crossed paths with Griggs even recently. It'll be a shame to eliminate all that raw talent.

Oh well.

Now to break the news to my very pregnant wife.

Nine hours later, I'm leaning against the wall on the second floor of an abandoned warehouse in New York. I sent Putnam an update of my ETA, and he said that all the materials would arrive shortly. I will say that seems to be the best part of doing jobs for the Brethren. They do all the heavy lifting. I don't need to stake out or hunt people down. They hand deliver them to me on a platter, I do what I do best, then I walk away with my bank account significantly padded. Even more so for this job. I wonder what the kid did to deserve such a high price on his head.

A shadow catches my attention from outside, and I stand at attention, adrenaline pumping in my veins. It's like a drug; one I will never tire of. The high that comes when you're on that edge of life and death is unlike anything else in the world, and when two people walk in and only one walks out, you can't help but feel like the ultimate victor.

I've grown accustomed to seeing clearly in the dark, but it's very clear that Griggs is taking a moment to adjust as he slips inside the warehouse, staying well within the shadows. Apparently he thinks he beat his target here. That's cute.

He clutches the duffle filled, no doubt, with his toys for the "job" he was sent on as he cases the place. I can't help but have a little fun with him. It would be a shame to see someone with so much potential go down before they even realized it.

I push the door to my right closed, allowing the soft snick to echo through the warehouse. Griggs's head whips up, but he clearly is still struggling to see me. Grinning, I reach into my pocket and pull out a throwing star. The smooth metal feels like silk between my fingers before I wind my arm back and let it sail through the room. I throw it a hair high, and it embeds itself in the wall beside his head.

He drops into a roll before popping up again as my heart begins to thunder in my chest. The hunt is on.

I pull more stars out and begin throwing them, one by one, each narrowly missing him, then drop down to the first level, landing almost silently as I throw my last star. I can tell Griggs is becoming frustrated that he can't see me, a knife on his hip and gun in his hand at the ready, but you can't kill what you don't see.

I pull out the gun from behind me, flick off the safety and fire a shot. The silencer keeps it quiet enough, only a soft whirr echoing through the warehouse. Griggs somehow expertly dodges it, impressing even me. I can't help but giggle as the euphoria of the kill is right at the tip of my finger.

Deciding someone with his skills deserves an honorable death, I do him a favor and step into the light. The instant he sees me, confusion clouds his face.

"Graves?"

I nod. Though he can't see the smile I'm giving him behind my mask, I know he can hear it in my words.

"You aren't too bad, Griggs. Better than your parents were, I'd say."

"Thanks," he practically spits. "Any particular reason you're trying to kill me?" he asks as I reach for my favorite knife, then swipe my hand out to plunge it inside him.

He lunges backward, his fist driving into my face before I

return the favor. He's within arm's reach now. If I wanted to be quick about it, he'd be bleeding out on the floor already, but I'm having too much fun playing. It's been a while since I've crossed paths with a worthy opponent.

Griggs's mind appears to be spinning, as if he's just put together that my target for the night is him. I take the opportunity to swing my knife out, catching his arm and slicing him open. The familiar feeling of blade tearing flesh runs through my knife and into my body like an electric zap I feel through every inch of my body. He grunts in pain as I deliver similar treatment to his other arm, forcing him to the floor.

The kid doesn't go down easy, though, kicking his leg out and knocking me down with him. Holy shit, I won't lie, that surprised me, and I can't help but bust up laughing at the thought that he just got me onto my ass. My head throbs from the impact, and I touch the back of it. My fingers come back wet and red.

"Nice one! You're a tough little fucker. Want a job?" I chuckle.

He huffs as we both jump to our feet. Blood pours from his arms and drips down my face. Then I make a move, and the gift it gives me is the feel of my blade sinking into his stomach. His breath is sucked out of him in an instant, and his eyes go wide with panic, like he's never considered actually dying on a job.

That's mistake number one. If you're not mentally prepared to die, you don't belong in this line of work.

He stumbles on his feet before slumping to the ground, blood pooling around him as his body begins to shake. That's it? The great Griggs legacy is going to die just like this? Shame.

I tsk at him, shaking my head in disappointment as I circle him.

"Vincent Griggs," I muse with a sigh. "Don't you remember the first rule of mercenary work? Strike fast and strike first. I was down! You almost had me!" I shout in excitement before sighing once more.

"I'm not gonna lie, I was kinda bummed when I heard you were my target. You've been fun to fuck with over the years, and you've got a lot of raw talent. A little coaching up and you could be a fucking animal."

I can see the fight is leaving him by the second, but he seems to be holding on with everything he has just to stay awake. He knows as soon as he's out, it's all over.

"I'm your target?" he rasps. "Who took the hit out?"

"You know as well as I, we just take orders," I lie, shrugging.

"And you know as well as I that you're a nosey fuck!" he tosses back.

Touché. If I didn't recognize Putnam's voice, I would have looked into it immediately. I don't blindly work for anyone.

I can't help but crack the fuck up. God, this kid is hilarious. I feel like in a different life we could have been great friends. I could teach him how to disembowel someone in under ten seconds, and he could lighten the fuck up. Seriously, he takes this line of work too seriously. I've never seen him crack a smile even once. You know what they say: if you love your job, you never work a day in your life.

Oh well.

"It was your boss," I say with a smirk. "Must have done something to piss him off. Then again, mine has gotten pissy if I didn't answer on the first ring. Maybe you don't deserve it, but business is business."

He attempts to lift himself, but where would he even go? He's not thinking rationally; he's just desperate.

I reach down and yank the knife out of his stomach, allowing blood to run like a river from him before lifting it up.

"Nice knowing you, Griggs."

"Please, Zayden!" he begs. "I got a girl," he says with a wheeze. "She's everything. Please. I can't leave, not when she'll be alone in this world."

I couldn't tell you what's gotten into me. Maybe it's that I'm becoming a father any day now. Maybe it's that I can picture myself in his position, moments from death, wanting nothing more than just one more smell of Blake's skin. That's the difference, though—I never would have gotten myself in his position. I don't lose. Ever.

I plunge the knife into his rib cage, shoving it all the way in before twisting it, then cup his head and push my forehead to his as I speak.

"Say hi to your mom and dad for me, kid."

With that, I rip the knife out of him, running the blood along my tongue as I watch him shake and gasp.

When I hear his phone ring in his pocket, curiosity gets the best of me and I fish it out, only to see a picture of a blonde girl with bright eyes smiling. Fuck. She kinda looks like Blake. I mean, my angel is perfect in every way and a smoke show in comparison, but the girl is pretty. I see what Griggs is all twisted up about.

I don't want to say what I do next is fueled by a conscience because we all know I don't have one. I tell myself it's an investment for the future. Fuck, I don't know.

I lean down, rip Griggs's shirt apart and staunch the stab wounds the best I can before I toss his phone to the side and pull out my own. I put the call on speaker as I hold pressure on the kid.

"I need a room. No cops, no questions," I say before lifting the kid into my arms and walking out of the warehouse.

"Got it," the voice says on the other end before the line goes dead.

Looking down at Griggs, I figure I'll give him this. A shot. If he makes it, he'll earn it. If not, then the job is complete all the same.

I'm texting Blake good morning and that I'm sorry I'm not there to wake her up when Griggs stirs in the bed before me. I pocket my phone and lean forward to watch him. His eyes slowly lift, and when he sees me, he groans.

"You're here. Means I didn't make the cut for heaven."

I smirk at that. "Are you surprised?"

"Not in the slightest."

Laughing at that, I nod as I wait for him. He takes in his surroundings, the bandaging around his torso, the IV, the monitors and the secluded hospital room tucked away into a corner of the hospital no one will be able to come to thanks to my contact.

"You... saved me," he says, more like a statement but with the hint of a question to it.

"Yeah."

"Why?"

I keep my mouth shut, mainly because I don't know how to answer him. I think over what to say or how to say it before I stand, taking a few steps towards his bed before I tilt my head to the side.

"You've got potential. You needed to live for your girl, and now... now you owe me."

"Owe you what?" he asks cautiously.

A wicked grin crosses my face. "Anything. A favor to be called in at anytime, anywhere, for anything. No questions asked."

He seems to think it over before he looks to me.

"I'm assuming this is non-negotiable."

I nod. "See what I said? Potential. We'll be in touch, Griggs. Whenever the mood strikes," I say as I begin moving to the door.

Before I step out, though, I pause.

"Oh, and if you wouldn't mind taking out your boss, that would be great. I've already reported the job complete and have been compensated. I don't need your little group coming after me for revenge."

"You mean the Brethren?" he asks.

I shrug. "Whatever you guys want to call yourselves."

Chapter One
Zayden

6 Years Later

"You worry too much," I say with a shake of my head.

"You don't worry enough," Dominic snaps, walking around to stand in front of me.

I shake my head and begin walking away when Dominic clutches my arm, pulling me back to face him.

"I'm serious, Zay. We have to come up with a plan."

I shrug him off and shake my head. "It's fine. We've taken precautions. The house is locked down. Our phones are back in Seattle. We're at a safe house for Christ's sake. What more do you want to do?"

"More! Our family is worth too much to leave anything to chance."

I look away from him and out to my angel on the beach. She's building sandcastles with Aries and Ryder. Well, she's building them with Ryder, and Aries is stomping them to pieces. I watch as Ryder leaps for him, tackling him to the ground before putting him into a headlock. We've been training the boys since they could walk, practically. Not to be killers but fighters. To hold their own, to protect themselves and their future brothers and sisters. Whenever it is Blake will let us have more, that is.

The twins' birth wasn't too terrible for her, though finding out that Ryder was in there was a surprise. He'd been hiding behind his brother during all of the ultrasounds, and it felt like the perfect kind of surprise. What came after was not so perfect.

She was hit with some serious postpartum depression that took her to a dark place. I was worried I'd never see light in my angel's eyes again. But we made it out the other side together, and she's the best mother, the best woman. We love our family, but it's no secret Dominic and I have been craving to add to it. As many as she'll allow us to have. Even I know better than to push her on it, though. It was... dark. She has to want it, and so we have to be patient.

The boys are six now. Growing up so fucking fast and absolute terrors. Ryder is quieter, steadier, but when his temper goes, it's a fucking force. Aries is more reckless. He's the act-first-and-think-later kid. I'm not saying he's a carbon copy of me at that age, but... yeah, he's me and then some.

They both got Blake's blonde hair, and both inherited Dominic's brown eyes. I refuse to believe that means he fathered them because we know it was obviously me. To be fair, one of my angel's eyes is brown too, so it's anyone's guess.

I feel myself smiling at them, my chest filled with so much peace and love I swear to God it's gonna burst. Turning to face my brother, I nod in agreement.

"What's the plan?"

"First, we need to establish where their resources begin and end. This isn't just anyone—this is the Four Horsemen. They're nasty sons of bitches. Why you took it on to begin with is beyond me."

"Not helping," I gnash at him as guilt eats away at me.

Mainly because he's right. We always swore we'd never get into bed with the Four Horsemen. They're nasty pieces of shit that Dominic and I met when Maxim adopted us. Two brothers and their two best friends. We went one way, and they went another, but while Dominic and I are organized, methodical, they're... reckless. I've seen Desmond go as far as to eat his kill afterwards, too high off the buzz of it all and just crazy enough to not let a single qualm get in his way. He makes me look like the goddamn Easter bunny.

The thought of them getting within even fifty feet of my family sends a chill down my spine. I'm not scared of anything or anyone, but seeing as I just killed Desmond and Dennis' sister—by mistake I'll add—yeah, they're out for our heads.

We haven't told my angel the extent of the danger we're all in. I didn't want to worry her, and also, she *knows*. She doesn't know the details, and she doesn't need them. One look at me and she didn't ask a single question, just quickly packed for herself and the boys, then we left Seattle within hours. We've been down in the Caribbean for three weeks now, and Dominic is beginning to go stir-crazy. He doesn't like to not be in control, and this situation... yeah, it's just fucked to shit. There is no control to be had.

"Tell me what to do and I'll get it done," I say.

Dominic nods as he heads inside, while my angel and the boys walk through the sand up to our house. We bought this place shortly after the boys were born. We thought it would be a nice vacation home... or a safe house. It felt excessive to buy an entire island, but after all those years of work, Dominic and I have saved up a nice chunk... more than a chunk. Anyways, this felt as good a place as any to go. It's completely untraceable—we literally paid to have it removed from all maps and radars. How Dominic pulled that off, I'll never know. Everything was done through shell accounts and offshore banking. It's as safe as we could possibly make it, which is why I know my brother is overreacting. Whatever he needs, I guess. He's right: our family is worth being absolutely sure. The sooner we take care of the Four Horsemen, the sooner we can all go home too.

"What are you two whispering about?" my angel teases as the boys chase after Dominic and she presses her lips to mine.

I'll never tire of her pillowy-soft lips. So perfect, and all mine.

Dominic steps in and steals her from my arms, cupping her face and crushing his lips to hers. She goes willingly, and I can't help but sulk.

Well, almost all mine.

After dinner, Dominic and I worked on pulling up any kind of connections the Four Horsemen could have, specifically in this area. We didn't find anything, which is equal parts relieving and unsettling. If we'd found something, I'd be comforted. Finding nothing means they've hidden it, and we're blind. We went to bed late and found my angel already asleep in the middle, where she always sleeps. I tucked her into my chest as Dominic wrapped himself around her, and we all drifted off into a perfect sleep.

Suddenly, screams echo through the house, forcing my eyes open in an instant. Dominic and Blake wake in the next moment as glass shatters in our room. Still half asleep, I reach beneath my bedside table, pull the gun taped under it and unload it into the intruder. He's not alone, though. Two more men dressed in all black jump through the opened window, one coming for me and the other for Dominic.

Another scream echoes through the house from the boys' room, and my angel's eyes fill with horror as she tears out of the room towards the screams.

"No! Stay here! I'll get them!" I shout as my attacker pulls a knife, slicing my arm. I yell before headbutting him.

After grabbing the knife from his hand, I snap his wrist in half before turning his arm and sinking the blade into his eye. He falls to the floor as I look to see Dominic beating his attacker to a pulp before I chase after Blake towards the boys.

My heart thunders in my chest as my legs stretch out, forcing myself to close the distance between me and them sooner. When I make it to the boys' room, I see a man pinning Ryder to the ground by his throat while Aries kicks and beats on his back. A second man is currently attacking my angel. Another one lies dead at our feet with a snapped neck.

That's my girl.

My boys and my angel—both need me, but I rush the man facing Blake just after he delivers a meaty punch to her face. She stumbles back as Aries cries out, "Mama!"

Thundering footsteps echo through the house before Dominic bursts in, gun drawn. He pulls the trigger and drops the man on top of Ryder to the ground before I grab a pair of scissors from the desk and force them into the neck of the man in front of me. His mouth drops open, and he stumbles back before Dominic fires off several rounds into his head. His body drops with a hollow thud, and the whole room goes quiet for a moment.

Then a choked sob rips out of my angel before she scrambles across the room to the boys and pulls them into her arms.

"Are you okay? Where are you hurt?" she asks Ryder before looking Aries over.

"I'm okay," Ryder insists, and Aries too gives him a once-over before his eyes move to his mom.

Her lip is split, and several parts of her face are already swelling. She looks back to us, anger and pain heavy in her eyes.

"Who the fuck was that?"

Dominic and I exchange uneasy glances before shaking our heads. We don't know who they were, but we sure as fuck know who sent them.

That's fucking it. This game of hiding out until we've gathered enough information is officially over. They hunted us down, preyed on us while our guard was lowered. They touched my family, and now I'm going to incinerate the goddamn world to burn those motherfucking rats out.

Slowly, my feet carry me to my angel and my boys. I press kisses to the top of each of their heads before holding Blake's face in my hands.

"I'm so sorry, angel. I promise: they will pay for this."

"Who?" she begs.

I shake my head, not wanting to involve her and the boys in this, but then I take a look around the room and understand how involved they already are. Because of me.

"We need to get out of here—now," Dominic says to me before looking to my angel.

"Where will we go? This is supposed to be our safe house, Dom!" she snaps in desperation.

An idea sparks in my head as I pull out my phone to make a call. It takes longer than is acceptable before a groggy voice answers the phone.

"Hello?"

"Remember that favor you owe me? I'm calling to collect."

Chapter Two
Vincent

A voice I haven't heard in six years echoes through my ears, capturing my attention in an instant.

"Remember that favor you owe me? I'm calling to collect."

Zayden Graves and the favor that's been looming over my head all this time. I've often wondered what it would be, what he would come up with as repayment for saving my life. For the devil himself showing compassion and kindness. I always knew it wasn't for nothing, that whatever favor he could command would be hell, and may even rescind that gift of life he gave me. It's like he said so many years ago, though. It's not like I really have a choice.

"What is it? The favor?" I ask, sitting further up in bed as I slip away from Skyla and walk towards the hall, so I don't wake her. Wesley immediately takes advantage of the space as Ronan is on her other side. Liam and Asher are in their room—probably sound asleep if the noises at two in the morning were anything to go off.

Everyone has their own room in the house, and the sleeping arrangements vary by the day. Sometimes Liam and Asher have the night alone; sometimes they're with Skyla. Sometimes Wesley and Ronan spend time alone. The constant is that I'm never without Skyla. It doesn't matter if I'm even in the bed—I'll sleep on the goddamn floor—but I refuse to not be in the same room as her. It's worked out over our last six years of marriage, and the others have come to accept it. That's what life in a relationship like ours looks like: when five men all have the same wife, you make compromises. Or should I say *they* make compromises. I'm non-negotiable.

Moving through the hall of our cabin, I'm careful to keep my voice low near Seraphina's room. She's just getting over a cold, and I don't want to wake her or the boys. We come out here every year the week before Christmas. It became a tradition after that first Christmas spent with Skyla.

"I'll update you in person. We'll be at your cabin in approximately eight hours."

The blood in my veins goes cold. Graves is coming here? To the cabin? With my family? Absolutely not.

"You can't—"

"C'mon, Ryder. Get your shoes on, baby. We need to hurry!" a woman's panicked voice sounds in the background.

I frown. Graves is with someone? He has a kid? I'm only assuming, but I could never picture the unstable hitman having a family, apart from his brother. My eyes move to the bay window, which showcases the couple of inches of new snow that's fallen overnight.

"My kids are here, Graves. Whatever you need can't involve them. I'll meet you somewhere else," I say.

"*My* kids are here. They need protection," he says through what sounds like clenched teeth.

"I'll get them out of here and then—"

"No one leaves. I'm gonna need you and all your brother husbands."

I wrinkle my face at that. Brother husbands? What the fuck?

"You've been watching me," I say flatly.

I hear rustling in the background before a bag is zipped shut.

"Of course. Eight hours, be ready to work. Oh, and put some fucking clothes on," he says before hanging the phone up.

I look down at myself, realizing I didn't get dressed when I slipped out of bed, then whip my head around the house. What the fuck? Does he have this shit bugged?

I take the stairs two at a time, banging on Asher and Liam's door before slipping back into Skyla's room.

Ronan and Wesley slowly lift their heads as Skyla stirs. Asher and Liam stroll leisurely into the bedroom, wiping the sleep from their eyes as Liam yawns.

"If you want me to suck you off, Vinny, you gotta let me wake up first."

I scoff as Asher shoves Liam's shoulder.

"We have a serious fucking problem," I say, earning alert gazes from everyone in the room.

"Wait, they're coming here? Like right now?" Asher asks.

I nod. "Yes."

"Well, we need to get the kids out of here, then," Ronan says as he goes to stand.

I shake my head. "Graves told me no one can leave."

Skyla frowns. "Why?"

I shake my head. "He said he needed... all of your help. I don't know what's going on. I've known him for years, and my parents knew him longer. He sounded... off. Not off in his psychopathic ways. He sounded... scared."

"Yeah, somehow you telling me the psycho killer who almost gutted you like a pig is feeling scared doesn't make me feel better," Liam scoffs. "I agree. We need to get the kids out of here. The rest of us can stay. Two of us can go with Sky and the kids—"

"He has this place bugged," I interrupt.

"I'm sorry?" Wesley asks with a raised brow.

Being the security expert of the group, this is definitely his department, and I fully intended beating the fucking shit out of him over it later.

"He could see me as we were talking. I was in the hallway."

Wesley climbs out of bed, slipping on a pair of boxers as Ronan does the same, then follows after him. My focus moves to Asher as he speaks.

"Do we trust this guy?"

"Fuck no," I spit.

"But he saved your life—there must have been a reason. And he called you for help. That doesn't sound like someone who wants to hurt you or your family," Skyla interjects.

I love my siren more than one soul could ever love another, but my sweet girl can be so naïve. So sheltered to how dark and depraved this world truly is. It's remarkable she's been able to hold on to some of that innocence considering the things that she's lived through.

I just shake my head before digging my hands through my black hair. I don't know what the fuck to do. Something in my gut tells me that it would cause us more harm to disobey Graves than it would to stay put, though.

"We'll put Skyla and the kids in the safe room until we've assessed everything properly," Asher says.

"Ash, I don't need to be kept away like a fragile doll," she snarks.

Liam reaches over to her, rubbing a soothing hand on her growing belly. "We know, babygirl. We're just trying to keep you and our babies safe, okay?"

She looks a little put out—she always hates being treated like the damsel in distress—but she's also reasonable. She understands that she's our entire fucking world, her and our kids. She knows that we're all overprotective and unapologetically so.

"Fine. I'm only agreeing because Ronan moved my favorite recliner in there and I miss it," she says as she pushes herself to stand.

"Where are you going?" I ask.

"To take a shower. Want to join me?" she offers.

I'd love to more than anything, but with the looming arrival of Zayden Graves and his family, there's so much I need to do. So much I have to prepare for. So I shove my hardening dick to the side and shake my head as I step out of the room.

Before the door shuts, I hear an enthusiastic Liam shout, "Count me in, babygirl!"

Chapter Three
Skyla

Liam practically sprints to the shower, turning on the water as a pair of arms sneak up behind me, wrapping around me before two large hands settle on my stomach.

"How's my little guy doing this morning, princess?" Asher rumbles into my ear, pressing gentle kisses to my neck as I smile.

"Good. He kept me up most of the night, though."

"Weird. His dad kept me up most of the night too!" Liam smirks as he strips down naked and slips into the shower.

"Liam," I say with a wrinkle of my nose. "Why do you have to make everything weird?"

He lets out a humor-filled laugh before popping his head out the shower door. "Life is funnier that way. Now get in here. I want to have a Skyla sandwich for breakfast!"

Asher scoffs but continues walking towards the shower before grabbing the hem of my sleep shirt. I lift my arms up as he slowly pulls it over my head. My eyes move to my reflection in the mirror, and I can't help but smile. I love being pregnant. Thank God for that too since these boys have kept me pregnant almost consistently since we went on our honeymoon. First we had Seraphina, who's now four. Then we had Jackson, who's three. Brooks is now two, and I'm five months along with baby number four. We haven't come up with a name yet, mainly because the more kids you have, the harder it is to come up with names you actually like.

Though we don't know for sure who any of the kids' biological fathers are, everyone likes to make their guesses. The current running one is that the baby I'm pregnant with now is Asher's. He made some grand scheme and got everyone out of the house for almost a full day while I was ovulating, and I swear to God we fucked on every surface of our home back in Salem.

Who knows if it really is, and honestly, I never want to know. We're all family, they're all Daddy and I think it works better that way. Of course, I'm nervous for school quickly approaching for Seraphina. Kids are mean, and it doesn't matter if your daddies practically run the entire Brethren—having five dads and one mom is a recipe for some little shit on the playground saying something.

Asher walks me into the shower, kissing up and down my neck as the warm water pours over me. I gasp at the relief on my already aching body as Liam grips the back of my neck and smiles, those green eyes flashing at me.

"Good morning, beautiful."

I smile as his lips meet mine, his tongue tangling with my own before he works his way down my body to settle between my thighs. He hmms, and I can practically hear his grin as he lifts one of my legs up and over his shoulder before running his tongue through me. I gasp at the feeling while one of Asher's hands comes to my nipple, gently pulling and rolling it between his fingers while his other hand moves down to my clit. Ash rubs tight, quick circles that have me shaking as Liam's tongue trails over me, circling around his fingers. They really are the best team in every way.

Liam slips a finger inside me before adding another, and I whimper as I squeeze around him. Asher chuckles into my ear, continuing to rub my clit as Liam feasts on me.

"Shh, just like that, princess. You're being so good for us."

I moan, resting my head against his shoulder as they continue to turn me into a wanting, pliable mess.

"Good boy—eat our wife's cunt," Asher praises.

Liam looks at him with an adoring smile, winking before nipping at my clit. I gasp at the feeling as he quickly licks and sucks the pain away. God, it's so good. Too good. I'll never get over having the amount of attention and pleasure my husbands provide me on a daily basis. I swear to God one day I'm going to die from it.

Death by orgasm. There are worse things, I suppose.

"Fuck, fuck, fuck, fuck," I moan through clenched teeth as I weave my fingers through Liam's golden hair, grinding my pussy against his face as Asher turns my head to face him.

"Come for us, princess. Cover his face with your cum."

My mouth drops open, and a moan escapes for half a second before Asher swallows it down, smashing his lips to mine as I ride wave after wave of my orgasm. It's so good, like a high I never want to come down from. Liam continues eating me until it's practically painful before I move away, letting out a shaky sigh.

Liam pulls away from me with a wet pop as he rises to his feet.

"Come taste our girl, Ash," he says before dragging Asher's mouth to his. I look up, smashed between them as their tongues tangle for dominance, both letting out soft moans of pleasure. Hands are everywhere, all three of us intertwined in an embrace of love and carnal need.

Asher bites down on Liam's lip so hard, it makes him grunt before pulling away.

"Bend over right fucking now," Asher commands, Liam being oh so willing.

Liam grabs the handles that Wes installed in the shower. Yes, I'm a woman with five husbands, four of whom occasionally fuck each other—my shower has specifically made sex handles.

Asher spreads Liam's ass, running his tongue through him

before pushing himself inside. Liam tenses at first before a pleasured moan escapes him. Asher slowly pulls out before pushing in again, working his cock deeper and deeper into Liam's ass.

"Goddamn, waking up with you two is the best way to start any day," Asher grits through his teeth.

"Agreed," Liam moans. "Get over here, babygirl. Come suck on me."

I take a seat on what Liam likes to call the cock sucker, which is basically a shower chair at the perfect height to suck dick—again, don't judge—before I reach out and slowly stroke him. Each of his piercings glint in the water, and Liam releases a shaky breath as I wrap my mouth around his head.

"Fuckkkk," he groans.

"There you go, princess. Just like that. Turn our boy into a mess."

I smile around Liam's cock, loving Ash's words as I push him deeper and deeper into my throat. We work together so effortlessly. So easily.

I feel Liam about to lose it, and Asher's jerky thrusts tells me he's close too. Reaching up, I begin massaging Liam's balls, practically pulling the cum out of them, and that's all it takes for him.

"Sky! Ash! Fuck!" he groans as his hips thrust towards me, shoving his cock deeper as the warm taste of his cum splashes against my tongue and down my throat.

Asher groans as he lets out his release a moment later, pushing himself as deep as he can into Liam.

When they're both finished, they let out slow breaths before we all pull apart. Both of them reach down, giving me a hand to help me stand, and I smile at them with appreciation. Our arms intertwine all of us as we stand in the warm water, soaking up this moment together.

Once we're finished actually getting clean, Asher and Liam both help me get dressed before doing the same. I'm not pregnant enough that I struggle with day-to-day tasks like putting shoes on or shaving my legs, but from the instant that test is positive, the guys won't let me lift a finger. I'd love to say it's too much and I wish they'd let me help, but I'm not a liar. It's the least they can do after I push out their huge babies through my vagina.

Seraphina was 7lbs 9oz, Jackson was 8lbs 5oz and Brooks was 9 motherfucking pounds and 6oz. I swear to God if this baby follows the trend of their brothers and sister, I'm getting a new vagina.

As we emerge ready for... God, I don't really know what kind of day we're going to have. Vincent seems nervous, which is concerning. He's never worried about anything. I don't know much about Zayden Graves. Only that he almost killed Vincent under Christopher's orders, only to turn around and save him. Other than that... he's a mercenary that Vincent and his parents knew, one with a terrible reputation. I was trying to be supportive before when I insisted on being there when he arrives with whoever he's bringing, but honestly, I'm more than fine to make sure my kids and I are safe.

When I walk down the cabin stairs, I find Jackson playing with his toy cars, Brooks watching some cartoon while sitting in Ronan's lap and Seraphina sitting on Vincent's hip as he rifles through the fridge.

Two heads of midnight-black hair and silver eyes look to me as I enter the kitchen. A smile crosses Seraphina's face, and a smirk appears on Vincent's, which is basically a grin for him. Okay, I know that I don't want to know who fathered which baby, but I have two eyes, and we all know the truth: Seraphina is definitely Vincent's.

The first girl born to an Elder family in over three hundred years. She's like a miracle, a sign that the curse has been broken, that the evil has been banished and the debt repaid. At least that's what my mother says it means.

When I told her and my father that we were having a girl, they both wept—they knew it meant so much more than just having a baby. They knew it meant that nothing would ever be as it was, in the best possible way.

Liam drops to the ground, grabs a few cars and begins playing with Jackson, making his drift around and of course adding all the appropriate sound effects to go along with it. Jackson laughs, lighting up when he sees Liam.

"You're a silly daddy," he says, smiling. Two big dimples pop through his chubby cheeks.

My heart turns to goo as I look at my family. It's big and loud and messy and so perfect.

I'm resting my hands on my belly when another pair come from behind me.

"Good morning, little one, and good morning to you, our littlest one," Wes says as he gets down onto his knees to talk to the baby.

I let out a laugh as I cup the back of his head and smile. Every baby has been "the littlest one" to Wesley, then when we get pregnant with another, they get promoted and given their own nickname.

"So what did you find? Is the place bugged?" Asher asks, catching Seraphina's and Jackson's attention.

I cut Asher a look as Seraphina turns her head.

"We have bugs?"

"No, baby," I say with a shake of my head. "Daddy's just being goofy." I smile before facing Asher and mouthing, "Not here."

Asher nods, running a hand through his hair as he and Wesley move down the hallway.

"What do you want for breakfast, siren?" Vincent asks.

"I want chocolate-chip pancakes!" Seraphina exclaims.

He lifts an eyebrow to her. "Does it look like I'm talking to you, little lady?" he asks before he starts tickling her. Infectious laughter fills the house as she squeals and giggles.

I laugh and nod. "Pancakes sound delicious. I'll help," I say as I move to grab the pancake mix.

"Absolutely not. Walcott, get up here and help!"

"Uh-oh, Daddy used the last name. I'm in trouble," Liam says with an exaggerated expression to Jackson, who giggles like it's the funniest thing.

"Go sit; we've got this," Liam says as he smacks my ass and presses a kiss to my cheek.

I smile and move over to the couch where Brooks is lying flat against Ronan's chest. That is until he sees me. He scrambles over to me, perching himself on my lap before readjusting himself to see the TV.

"Easy on the baby, Brooks," Ronan says gently.

The two-year-old isn't too happy about not being the littlest anymore, and his back pushing into me is proof of that.

I shake my head and smile at Ronan. "He's okay."

Ronan nods as he closes the distance between us, wrapping an arm around my shoulders. "And how is Mommy doing this morning?"

I look up at him and smile. "Good. How is Daddy?"

He flashes me a look that promises nothing but the naughtiest things as he moves his mouth to my ear. "Daddy would be better if Mommy was sitting on his face."

My cheeks heat up as I look to make sure Brooks can't hear us. When I see he's completely zoned out, I move my mouth to Ronan's ear.

"Maybe we can sneak away after breakfast and see about that."

Ronan shoots me a wink, pulling me closer into him as Asher and Wes reappear. I hear soft whispers coming from the kitchen before Seraphina and Jackson join me on the couch. Ronan then stands and joins Asher and Wes, who exchange hushed conversation and worried glances.

A nervousness hangs in the air, and it feels justified. None of us know what to expect. All we can do is... hope, I guess.

Chapter Four
Dominic

This is a bad idea. I don't know why Zayden would even consider this. I spent the entire plane ride here researching these people within an inch of their life, and I still don't feel good about this. We're in no position to judge their relationship, but these guys are the heads of one of the country's most powerful secret societies. Scrap the country—the world. They're nearly untouchable, and we really think they're going to be okay with us waltzing into their vacation cabin with their kids a week before Christmas? Yeah, Zayden may say I worry too much, but once again, he isn't worrying enough.

Zayden chose to drive when we landed in New Hampshire. It's currently dumping snow, and I have to be thankful that we landed when we did because otherwise, I'm not confident we would make it to their cabin before the snow buries the road altogether.

Now I'm sitting in the front seat with Blake and the boys in the back. Silently, I'm pre-loading several guns, enough for all of us, even the boys. They've been going to the shooting range we've set up at our house for a year now. It's not an ideal situation to hand two six-year-olds guns, but I'm not sure what we're walking into, and if it gives them a small chance to live, then so be it.

I feel a pair of eyes on me, and I cut my gaze to the rearview mirror to see Blake staring at me with concern, those entrancing blue and brown eyes shining with emotion. I do my best to give her a comforting smile, but I know I don't succeed.

We're all more than a little rattled. We've never had our home invaded like that, not since the boys were born. I feel like I've failed them all. I should have anticipated it, acted quicker. Ryder and Aries haven't spoken a word since we got on the plane, and I worry that our choices will affect them forever.

"Are we sure this is the best option?" Blake asks from the back.

Zayden and I look back to her as she looks down at the boys.

"I just... Are we sure this is what we should be doing?"

I look to Zayden, who hesitates for a moment before nodding.

"Yes. We need to get somewhere safe, with high security. Some-where we can't be linked to."

I scoff and shake my head as I continue loading clips. High security my ass. It took almost no effort at all to hack into their surveillance feed over six years ago, and clearly they never suspected a thing. Zayden asked me to tap into all their properties and leave the link open should the need ever arise to use it. To my knowledge, he's only popped in a time or two over the years. I gotta say, I'm grateful for it now.

I look down at my phone and scroll through the different rooms. Right now, it looks like almost all of them are in the living room watching a show. Until I see the girl, Skyla, stand and take the kids with her down the hall. I try to follow them, but in the next moment she's gone. Furrowing my brows, I begin flicking through all the possible cameras before locking my phone.

"What?" Zayden asks.

"The girl and kids disappeared."

"What do you mean?"

I shrug. "Probably a safe room hidden by a corner or something."

"Does that mean we should be concerned?" Blake asks.

I turn to gaze over my shoulder and see the boys' eyes looking to me in concern. But I have no concern; there's no room for it. No one will hurt my family—not again, not ever.

"No," Zayden and I answer simultaneously.

Blake looks at me like she doesn't believe me, and I don't blame her. She knows us well enough to know when we're lying or trying to pacify her. She absolutely fucking hates it, but right now, she doesn't seem to take much issue with it. Instead, she places a kiss to each of our boys' heads as we start up the rural road to the cabin.

"I love you," I mouth to her.

She softens slightly, that smile that still makes my heart clench gracing her face as she mouths back, "I love you more."

I never could have imagined winning the love of a woman like her. Our story isn't cut and dry, though; it's messy, complicated and, probably to most, fucked up. But I wouldn't trade it for the world. She's my everything. *They* are my everything.

As we crest the last bend, the cabin comes into view. Of course, I've already studied it extensively, from the property lines and blue-prints to the interior photos the real estate company posted when it was for sale. Still, the place is fucking massive. I suppose it would have to be if you had six adults and three kids. This is just one of their vacation homes too.

Zayden turns his head to face Blake and the boys before he speaks. "Stay here. Dominic or I will come get you. If you hear shots, you drive away, you hear me? You drive and you never look back."

Blake shakes her head in protest as I cut in.

"Baby, yes. Our first priority is you three. You will get to safety, okay?"

She looks conflicted as the boys gaze up at her, then us. In the next moment, Ryder unbuckles his seat belt and throws himself around my and Zayden's necks. We both hold him close, pressing kisses to his head.

"We're gonna be okay, Ry, I promise," I whisper into his ear.

He nods as he pulls away, then Aries does the same. We both offer Blake a confident nod before I grab a few guns, passing them to Zayden before holstering my own, then giving one to Blake as well. She takes it easily, shooting me a worried look before Zayden and I climb out of the car together.

We make our way up to the front door of the cabin, our heads constantly swiveling for the slightest indicator that something may be off. When we approach the door, Zayden looks to me, checking to see if I'm ready. I nod as he lifts his hand to knock.

Knock—can you believe it? I don't think he's knocked on any door a single day of his life.

Slowly, the door opens to reveal Vincent Griggs standing in the doorway.

"Graves," he says with a nod to Zayden before turning to me. "Other Graves."

I scowl at that as Zayden lets out a laugh I think is supposed to sound amused but really just sounds maniacal.

"I told you I liked this kid, Dom."

I grunt in response as I stare him down. He meets my gaze when I cock my head to the side.

"Well? Are you going to let us in or what?"

"Why did you want to come here?" Griggs asks, turning his focus back to Zayden.

"You know, I've just been really feeling the need to get together with you, catch up. You got any beer?"

Griggs remains impassive, refusing to feed into Zayden's bull-shit for one second. Hm, maybe Zayden is right. I kinda like this kid too. Doesn't mean I trust him, though.

"Let us in and we'll explain as much as we're able," I say.

"How do I know you won't blow my family's brains out the moment I widen this door?"

"How do we know the same?" I throw back.

Griggs narrows his eyes and clenches his jaw. Finally, he relents, giving a shaky nod before pulling the door open.

"Thank you, good sir," Zayden says with a dramatic bow, stepping in first.

I follow right behind him, clocking each of the remaining men. Two Putnams, one Walcott and a Preston. They all appear armed and guarded, ready to attack. That makes two of us.

"This is—" Griggs begins before I cut him off.

"No need for introductions; we know who you all are. Where are Skyla, Seraphina, Jackson and Brooks?"

Mentioning the names of their woman and children sets them all off, and predictably Asher Putnam is the first to step toe to toe with me, pushing his gun against my stomach.

"What the fuck did you just say?"

I look at the impassioned hothead and roll my eyes. This is the leader of the Brethren? Seems like an ill fit, but what do I know about running a secret society?

Zayden tsks. "Dominic, don't set our hosts off like that." He smiles to the room before his gaze settles on Asher. Zayden's friendly demeanor vanishes in a moment.

"I suggest you remove the gun pressed against my brother before I cut out your entrails and shove them down your goddamn throat."

That seems to catch Asher off guard; he turns to Zayden, visibly disgusted.

"What the fuck?"

Griggs sighs and shakes his head. "Look, Graves, we're just trying to protect our family, same as you. The sooner you tell us what you want, the sooner we can all go about our lives."

Zayden looks to me before speaking. "The Four Horsemen are

after us. A job went south with them, and nine hours ago, they tracked down our safe house and attacked us. We need a safe place to keep our family so we can take care of them properly."

"And fast," I add.

Everyone in the room seems to relax a bit as Ronan Putnam speaks.

"So that's it? You just need us to look after your wife and kid?"

"Kids," I correct.

"And no," Zayden says as his gaze turns to Griggs. "We'll be requiring your handy-dandy hitman as well. Maybe a few others if you can hold your own."

"And if we say no?" Asher asks.

I look to him, surprised at his boldness, before reaching for Walcott. He tries to fight me off, but I subdue him easily, pressing my gun to his temple. In an instant, every weapon is drawn on me, but I don't care. I see the look of fear in Asher's eyes as I hold hostage the man he loves.

"Then I suppose this will turn into one big turkey shoot."

"Enough with the dick measuring," Ronan grinds out. "Let Liam go, and we can discuss what you need further."

"As a matter of fact, hand over your guns," Wesley adds.

Zayden lets out an amused laugh and shakes his head. "That's not happening, but we will lower our guns in good faith. Right, brother?" he says as he holsters his gun and raises his hands in surrender dramatically.

I push Walcott to the side and do the same, securing my weapon before I lift my hands. Zayden and I don't need to converse to understand the situation here. They don't trust us as much as we don't trust them, but they don't want a fight any more than we do. The woman they love and their children are here, same as us. They're a neutral threat for now, which is good enough for me.

Once our weapons are lowered, Griggs lowers his gun before

looking to the others. Slowly, they all do the same, Asher being the last to finally do so.

"Well, now that we have the warm and fuzzy greetings out of the way, how about you go get your family and we'll get ours. Make the kids feel more comfortable and all," Zayden tells—not asks—them.

I see several hesitations before Ronan and Wesley nod, then disappear down the hallway that I watched Skyla vanish from.

"I'll go get them," I say to Zayden.

"Sounds good! We'll play catch-up while you're gone!" He grins, waving to me like a fucking psychopath.

Asher and Liam give him uneasy looks before I hear Griggs and Zayden begin discussing our situation.

When I step out of the house, a door is thrown open, and Aries runs for me, Ryder close behind him and then Blake, yelling at them to get back.

I crouch down and scoop the boys up. "Did you forget that I said to wait in the car?"

They both look down, rightfully ashamed as Blake comes up to me, shaking her head.

"I swear to God they only listen to you two."

She pauses for a moment, looking for Zayden. "Is everything okay?"

I nod. "For now. Don't lower your guard, but for now, we're okay."

Blake blows out a breath and nods as I lean in to press a quick kiss to her lips. She melts against me before I pull away, setting the boys down and taking her hand in mine.

When we step inside the house, I have the boys tucked behind Blake and me as all eyes swing to us. Four new pairs of eyes are among them, all watching with varying levels of hesitancy. One seems to capture the attention of the boys, though.

Before we can stop them, Aries sprints forward, followed by Ryder, until they're inches from Seraphina, the family's four-year-old.

"What's your name?" Aries asks.

She looks at him nervously before glancing at her mom, who gives her a small nod. "Seraphina. What's yours?"

"I'm Ryder," he says, pushing in front of his brother.

Aries shoulder-checks him so that he's front and center once more. "I'm Aries."

She nods, still watching the boys with bright gray eyes like she's unsure of them.

"Do you want to play?" Jackson, the family's three-year-old asks.

Aries and Ryder nod as they take off with Jackson, running towards the back of the cabin, Brooks toddling behind them.

Aries pauses, looking back. "C'mon, Seraphina."

Now she looks to her dad, or so I'm assuming, since the girl appears to be a spitting image of Griggs. He's frowning at her like he doesn't approve before Skyla places a hand on his shoulder and nods to her daughter.

"Go play, baby. We're going to talk about grown-up stuff."

She nods and trails after them. None of us miss how Aries grabs hold of her hand the instant she's close enough, leading the way like this is his house or something.

"Oh Christ," I mutter under my breath.

Zayden casts me a look as a laugh bubbles out of Blake.

"Um, I think my boys are taken with your daughter."

Skyla laughs, nodding as she closes the distance between her and Blake. She holds her hand out. "I'm Skyla."

Surprise flickers in Blake's eyes as she nods before taking her hand. "Blake."

Skyla smiles warmly at Blake, and I watch closely for a hint of malice or deceit, but I come up empty.

"So how do we kill these Horsemen fucks and get you all out of here?" Asher asks.

"Ash," Skyla hisses, whipping her head round to face her asshole of a husband.

Zayden seems to be amused by it, though, as he cackles a laugh and nods. "He's right. Let's dive into it."

Chapter Five
Blake

It was hard at first trying to keep track of everyone's names. The introductions were brusque and, apart from Skyla and Liam, devoid of any warmth. Which, I'll admit, I can't blame them for. I mean, if the roles were reversed, I doubt the guys would be welcoming strangers into their kids' home with open arms. Still, I think that's the piece that gives us all comfort. We have equally precious things to lose here. It's like for now, in this house, we're Switzerland or something.

Honestly, though, five husbands? I'm not judging, not in the slightest. It's just... I thought I was a little out there with my two husbands. Granted, they're twins, so maybe that amps up the taboo factor a touch? But I'm pretty sure I caught that Asher and Ronan are nephew and uncle, so I don't really know. All I can say is Skyla definitely has her hands full. The house full of kids and one more on the way is a clear indication of that.

Again, not judging. Just... observing.

Eventually, Skyla and I slipped away to watch the kids play in the playroom. I was getting anxious not having my eyes on the boys, and I think she could tell. She's younger than me by at least ten years, but she has this calm presence about her, so you wouldn't know it.

"So you guys are from Seattle?" Skyla asks as she sits down and looks to me.

Slowly, I take a seat too, glancing over one more time to see Aries and Ryder playing tag with Seraphina, narrowly missing stomping on the littlest one each time.

"Careful!" I hiss to them before turning to her. "Yeah, Seattle. You?"

"Salem, Massachusetts. My husbands grew up there, but I actually grew up in London."

"London? Shit, that's really cool."

She smiles softly and nods. "It is. My aunt still lives there, and we try to visit at least once a year."

I nod before my gaze drifts to a blank wall and more thoughts than I'm able to control envelop me.

"Hey," she says, snapping me out of my daze. "Are you okay?"

"Me? Yeah, I'm fine. I've dealt with worse, trust me," I say, shrugging her off.

She nods in understanding before tilting her head to the side. "I'm sure you have. You seem like a strong woman, but... you were attacked in a home that was designed to be safe. Your children were attacked. It would be understandable if you were a little... shaken."

I look to her hesitantly. What's her angle? Why is she being so nice to me? Is this part of their plan? Are they looking for some kind of information? Something they can use against the guys? Against us? I—

"I'm sorry," she says with a shake of her head. "I'm prying. I tend to do that. We don't have to talk about it. I just... I'm sorry you went through that. That your boys did. You'll all be safe here."

I give her a tight smile and nod, appreciating the sentiment but desperately wanting to evade this topic.

"So," she begins again, like she doesn't have it in her to simply sit in silence. "Twin brothers?"

She's smirking at me with intrigue, and I can't help the laugh that bubbles out of me as I nod.

"If you're wondering how great it is... it's better."

She laughs at that. "I can only imagine. I don't think I've ever met another poly couple before."

"We're not really poly; we're just... us."

Skyla smiles at that, nodding softly. "I get that. I'm not sure I'd call us poly either. We're just... in love," she says simply.

I nod and give her a small smile. "How do the kids do with five dads?"

She shrugs. "I'm sure the same that your boys do with two. They don't know what it's like not to have five dads constantly worrying over them, ready to play, to hold them. To be honest, they're all downright spoiled with attention."

"I was playing with her first!" Ryder snaps.

"Too bad. She's having more fun with me!" Aries throws back.

Skyla and I share a look before busting up laughing.

"It looks like your daughter won't lose any attention while we're here," I say.

"Oh no, look at her—she's absolutely eating it up," she replies, pointing to her daughter, who's standing between my boys like she's queen of the world.

You go, little queen.

In the next moment, a figure comes into the room, dropping down behind Skyla. She startles for a moment before smacking Liam's arm.

"Don't scare me like that, asshole!"

He snickers, placing kisses against her neck before smiling at me. "How's it going in here?"

I smile. "Good. The boys are infatuated with Seraphina."

"As they should be—she's the best." He beams with pride.

"How's it going out there?" Skyla asks.

"Oh you know, my dick is bigger than yours. I have a better plan. No, I do," he says, imitating each person's voice absolutely terribly.

"Awesome," Skyla sighs.

"But I come with good news. Wesley and I are starving—"

"What's new?" Skyla scoffs.

"Ah, rude," Liam throws back before smiling. "I was going to run out and pick up some provisions. Anything the boys like in particular?"

The gesture is surprisingly kind, and it settles a piece inside of me. Shaking my head, I smile. "Whatever you get, they'll eat. Thank you."

"Alright! I'll be back soon," he says, pressing a kiss to the top of Skyla's head before he practically bounces out of the room.

"He's got... a lot of energy," I say slowly.

Skyla laughs, nodding in agreement. "That he does."

Chapter Six
Ronan

Liam brought home a mountain of food—tacos and burritos. Typically, our takeout orders are large because we have nine mouths to feed, but this is insane. Seven takeout bags later, the kitchen island and dining room table are covered, every inch, with food of some sort. All the kids are eating burritos decently in peace until Liam flicks a spoonful of beans at Jackson. He gives Liam a wicked smile as he does the same, nailing him right in the forehead. Naturally, the Graves twins think this is hilarious and begin grabbing handfuls of food, tossing them at anyone and everyone. When Brooks gets an eyeful of sour cream, I decide to call it.

"Alright, we're done. Enough!" I snap at Liam, who's still throwing food.

He pauses, looking at me with a guilty smile. Rolling my eyes, I smack the back of his head as I take a bite of my food and point my fork at him. "You're a bad influence, so you'll be cleaning up this mess."

Liam's eyes go wide the way the kids' do when they're outraged by something. "C'mon—that's not fair. I was just messing around!"

"Liam, you're almost twenty-eight years old," Skyla scoffs, laughing as she shakes her head.

He shrugs like he couldn't care less how old he is before he starts eating some of the food on the table. The Graves twins grin before they begin doing the same. Seraphina watches them carefully before going back to her own meal.

"I need a drink," I mutter as I stand.

"Get me one too, Daddy!" Liam calls out.

"No," I answer flatly. "Blake? Would you like something? Beer? Wine? Tequila?"

Skyla laughs as Blake shakes her head.

"No, thank you."

"You sure?" I ask as I pour myself a Scotch.

She pauses for a moment before giving me a smile that doesn't quite reach her eyes. "I'm okay. Thank you, though."

I nod as I take my seat once more, wrapping my arm around the back of Skyla's chair as she and Blake dive into talking about growing up in Chicago, where Blake's originally from, versus London. The kids are all shouting and laughing. Things feel good in this moment. At least, I think I'm supposed to feel that way. I can't help this gnawing sensation in the pit of my stomach that we've welcomed a shitstorm by opening the door to them all. Though, if what Vincent says is true, and the Graves brothers' reputations bear no falsities... I'm not sure we would have made it had we turned them down.

A pair of hands come to rest on my shoulders, massaging them and startling me.

My eyes land on the culprit. Wesley of course.

"You okay, Ro?"

I nod as he chuckles, lowering his mouth to my ear.

"You need to relax. Everything will be okay. They seem to be in a bind, and there are more of us than them. We don't need to worry—"

"It's my job to worry," I hiss back at him, causing Blake and Skyla's conversation to cease.

I give them an apologetic look before turning to look up at Wesley, who's continuing to knead my shoulders. He stares down at me with one eyebrow lifted in challenge.

"Sorry," I mutter before shaking my head.

Once again, he leans down to whisper to me, his lips dragging against my ear as he does.

"You're only allowed to speak to me like that in the bedroom. Anywhere else, unacceptable."

I turn to see no irritation or frustration on his face. Instead, he's giving me a goading smile like he wants me to argue or fight back just so he can prove me wrong.

"Later," I say lowly, causing a smile to curve Wesley's lips as Skyla moves to stand. We both look towards her as she starts off towards the garage.

"Where are you going?" I ask.

"The kids want more juice, and we ran out in the house."

"I'll get it," I say and stand, following after her.

"It's fine, Ronan," she calls over her shoulder as she continues.

She steps through the threshold into the garage as I quickly follow behind her, looping my arms around her and pulling her back to me.

"You need to slow down. That's what we're all here for—things like this."

She smiles, shaking her head as she looks up at me. "You're not my servants, and I'm perfectly capable of grabbing some juice."

I spin her around to face me, slipping one hand behind her neck as my gaze drills into hers. "It's not about what you're capable of, baby. We all know you're capable of so much. You're incredible. It's about letting us take care of our wife, the mother of our children, the love of each of our lives."

She smiles at me softly before lifting her hand and cupping my cheek. Her fingertips brush against the side of my eyes, where my age is absolutely starting to show. I'm over ten years older than her, and while that's by no means old, I feel the stresses of our life catching up to me. I know that I'll go gray in no time. Skyla and Wes both say they can't wait for me to be a silver daddy. I, however, have reservations about such things.

"You're worried," she states.

"Of course. There are strangers in our home, in our winter cabin. They're at our table, with our kids. Everything feels extremely out of control thanks to Griggs."

Skyla's eyes narrow at me as her hold on my face stiffens. "You're seriously blaming this on Vincent? He was given a choice: life with a favor or death. He chose life; he chose me. He chose... How can you say that?"

I know she's right, but goddamnit, I need someone to blame. I need something to fix. I can't be this useless. I'm the fixer—I put things back together; I find solutions. Right now, I can't do shit, and it's driving me fucking crazy.

"I'm sorry. I know—I know it's not his fault. I just..." I trail off, shaking my head when I feel Skyla pull my face to hers.

I go easily, like I always do. With Skyla, there's never any choice: being near her, it's like breathing for the first time in what feels like forever. It's relief and peace and undiluted bliss.

Her lips brush mine, and slowly, the tension in my shoulders eases, at least for a moment. Her tongue swirls against my own, and I pull back, resting my forehead against hers.

"What are you looking to start here, baby?"

She blinks up at me, her big, beautiful green eyes staring at me with the picture of innocence, but that's not what her dirty fucking mouth conveys.

"Just trying to relieve Daddy's stress. Is it working?"

My cock hardens in an instant at that, a low growl rumbling in my chest.

"You want Daddy to fuck you, baby?"

Skyla's teeth sink into her lower lip as she nods. In half a second, I'm on my knees, yanking down her leggings and tossing them to the other side of the garage before my face is buried between her legs.

Her gasp is sharp as she buries her hand in my hair, pulling me closer as she moans. "Oh fuck!"

My tongue swirls around her clit as she pants and wiggles against me. She tastes so goddamn sweet. Like my favorite treat that I could never tire of.

I release her with a wet-sounding pop and stand, pulling my cock out of my pants before lifting her up into my arms. I sink her down onto me slowly, and she mewls as she tosses her head back.

"Shhh," I mutter as I rest my forehead against hers. "We have company. You don't want the Graves brothers to find Daddy fucking you, do you?"

She whimpers at that, shaking her head.

"Stay quiet for me, baby. We're gonna make this nice and fast," I say as I begin slowly thrusting into her, picking up speed with each thrust until we're both fucking feral.

I take a few steps towards the wall and press her against it so I have better control. Once her back is flush, I roll my hips, pushing the head of my cock against her G-spot in a way that has her eyes fluttering.

"Oh my—"

I cut her words off by pressing my mouth against hers, and our tongues battle for dominance as I continue fucking her against the wall. All I can hear is heavy breathing and the sound of skin against skin.

We haven't done anything this risky in quite some time. Any number of people could come out here and catch us. We should have at least locked the door or something, but there's no stopping now.

My cock throbs inside her, and I know my release is coming soon. Pulling back, I quickly begin rubbing tight circles against her clit as I murmur into her ear. "Hurry, baby. I want to feel you come on my cock."

"Oh God," she whimpers as I move my fingers faster and faster against her. "Shit! Fuck! Daddy," she cries out, not at all quietly enough, but it's what I need to fall over the edge.

My cock jerk as I shoot my cum into her. I thrust deeper and deeper, as if I could get her pregnant with a second baby right now. Fuck, I'd love nothing more.

Since we married Skyla, we've pretty much kept her pregnant —not that she's complaining per se. I think we've all developed a breeding kink, and with five dads, there's no telling if or when we'll stop.

Suddenly, the door opens, and my heart seizes in my chest. Adrenaline pumps through my veins at the idea of being caught as I quickly shield Skyla.

"What is taking so lon—?" Wesley starts before cutting himself off. "Fuck, I knew I should have come with to grab the juice," he says as his eyes meet mine.

I scoff as I slowly pull Skyla off me, setting her down to her feet before grabbing her leggings and slipping them back on for her.

"Did you destress Daddy, little one?" Wesley teases as Skyla smirks, shooting him a wink.

"Doing what I can. You're up next."

"Challenge accepted," he says, rubbing his hands together mischievously.

I let out a rough laugh as I shake my head at both of them, then lean down to press a kiss to Skyla's lips.

"I love you," I say.

She smiles up at me. "I love you too."

When I turn, Wesley is there, cupping my face and stealing a kiss before I can even breathe. As he pulls away, his eyes are heavy on mine, so many words swimming just below the surface, so many things practically begging to spill out. They don't, though, because I'm not ready. Or I don't know how to be ready. I don't really know. I never saw what Wesley and I have coming, and I've never known how to handle it. It's not as easy for us as it was for Asher and Liam. Or maybe I should say it's not as easy for me. Wesley and I are more carnal, lustful over love.

That's what I keep trying to convince myself at least.

Chapter Seven
Vincent

We've been working nonstop since they got here, with no end in sight. Zayden and Dominic fight worse than Asher and I do, and that's saying something because our distaste for each other ran deep. Still does when he's being an arrogant prick.

I look at the clock to see that it's long past the kids' bedtime, which means Skyla is either already in bed with one or all of the others, or crashed out. I want nothing more than to toss my hands up, call it a night and climb in beside her. I always sleep best when her head is resting against my chest, the soft sounds of her breathing calming me like my own personal sound machine.

I can't, though. We have to come up with a plan—and fast. I've only heard rumors of the Four Horsemen, much like the Graves brothers. They're practically urban legends, though according to Zayden, they're very real and worse than I imagined.

"I just don't understand why you would've taken a job from them if they're that bad?" Asher scoffs, yet again showing his dickish side.

I've tried to advise him several times to watch his mouth, but he doesn't listen. If he gets stabbed, that's on him.

The knife that Zayden is twirling in his hands stills, conveniently pointed in Asher's direction as he tilts his head to the side. "You're right, Griggs. He is a mouthy little shit."

Asher scoffs, like Graves doesn't intimidate him. Yet again, his arrogance is blinding because if he knew what I knew, he would be intimidated.

"I'm just saying, you get called on a hit or whatever by the Four Horsemen, you say yes. I can't see why you didn't question it when it was the leader's little sister's boyfriend? Or did you not do enough research?"

Dominic shoots his brother a look and throws out an arm, stopping Zayden as he lunges, the knife in his hand inches from Asher's left eye.

Zayden gives him an eerie smile that transforms his face into something out of a horror movie.

"You can't see? Let me take a look at your eyes," he says as I reach out and grab his other hand, which is now holding another knife, stopping it mere inches from Asher's right eye.

Dominic and I hold Zayden the best we can as he shakes against us, his strength almost too much. All the while he holds that calm and creepy smile.

Asher seems to finally understand the magnitude of the people we're dealing with as he roughly swallows before lifting his head like the "fearless leader of the Brethren" that he is.

"Sorry," he mutters as he looks down at his phone and begins typing out some kind of message.

Dominic whispers something into his brother's ear, and Zayden struggles against us once more before roughly pushing back, retaking his seat and propping his legs onto the desk in our security room. Dominic watches his brother for another moment before resuming his work on Wesley's computer. It took him all of two seconds to gain access and begin utilizing every resource the Brethren has at their disposal.

"So, the plan?" Asher asks, clearing his throat.

I cut him a look, and he shrugs at me before turning back to the brothers. Dominic continues typing as Zayden goes back to playing with his knife, keeping his eyes on Asher this time.

"Take them out," Dominic says.

"If they're supposed to be so formidable, how do you anticipate achieving that?" Asher asks.

I sigh, Dominic shakes his head and Zayden cackles, though his smile quickly turns into a glare as he speaks.

"By taking them out one at a goddamn time, pretty boy. Why the fuck is he in here?"

"Our latest intel wasn't even close to tracking down Desmond, but the others are much more... sloppy. Augustus will be the easiest to find."

Zayden snorts in agreement.

"Why is that?" I ask.

"Because he goes through hookers like a tweaker sifts through the trash. He finds them, fucks them and leaves a trail of bodies through whatever city he's in," Zayden scoffs.

"How is that going to be easy to—?"

"Got him," Dominic says, interrupting Asher, thank fuck. "Looks like he was in Toronto as early as last week. Two missing women have been reported in Buffalo, New York, this afternoon. We'll leave in a few hours." He copies and pastes something, then emails it to himself before wiping the account.

I cut him a look as he stares back at me, waiting to see if I'll question him.

"Excellent. What do you need from us?" Asher asks.

"Besides keeping our entire world protected?" Dominic asks before looking at Zayden.

He looks up at the ceiling like he's thinking over this request with great detail. "Restock of weapons, hourly proof of life of our family, unlimited access to your intel and him," he says, pointing at me.

Asher looks to me, as if we have a say. As if this is a negotiation before I look to Zayden and nod.

"Done."

Asher and I showed Dominic and Zayden their room for the night, and they went to bed as Asher got a phone call. He cursed at it before stepping back into the security room to take it. He handles a lot of Brethren shit that I don't care to know or think about. If it wasn't for Skyla and her insistence that she loved the others, I'd have stolen her away a long time ago. I still think about slipping her and the kids a sedative and all of us making a getaway to somewhere warm, tropical and remote, where no one will ever find us. She'd hate it, though, and she'd hate me. So, despite it going against every cell in my body, I tolerate the rest of them for her and now for the kids.

I step into Skyla's bedroom, my eyes taking in the scene before us in an instant. Liam and Wesley are naked, tumbling around on one side of the bed as their tongues wrap around one another, while Skyla is bouncing on Ronan's cock, facing Wesley and Liam—to watch I assume. All four eyes land on me before their actions resume. I really wanted to get some time alone with my siren before I have to leave in a few hours. An orgasm and a little bit of sleep with her on top of me will have to do, I suppose.

The smile Skyla sends me forces my heavy heart to thunk to life. It only beats for her and the kids, just the way it was intended to. It may be in my body, but it's always been hers. From the moment I laid eyes on her, I stopped existing for myself and became completely and unashamedly hers.

Skyla is naked, her breasts bouncing gently as she rolls her hips on top of Ronan while she faces me. I cup the side of her face as she smiles up at me, my thumb dragging against her lip as she sucks it into her mouth. Fuck.

Her tongue twirls and sucks on my thumb as my cock instantly stiffens in my pants. With my free hand, I quickly undo them, stroking my cock a few times before lining myself up to her mouth. She bends down slightly so she's able to take me before I push myself into her mouth and down her throat.

She gags and squirms, but I push forward just a little more, needing her to take every fucking inch of me. My head lolls back as her mouth pulls off me before pushing back down once more. Weaving my fingers through her silky blonde hair, I let out a deep groan as her tongue swirls around me, leaving a spit-covered layer over the tattoo I have for her on my cock. I got that done before we got married; had been thinking about doing it from the moment I first stroked my cock to the thought of her. I knew right then and there that it was all for her, and how better does one show that than to ink it into their skin forever?

"That's a good girl," Ronan praises. "Choke on his dick while you ride mine."

Skyla moans at his words, taking us both with a new vigor. I continue thrusting myself down her throat when the door opens, Asher standing in the doorway with a disappointed frown.

"Fuck you all. Couldn't have waited for me?" he grouches.

"We started long before you were done," Wesley replies, grinning as he pulls away from Liam.

Asher continues grumbling like a toddler as he kicks off his shoes and slowly gets undressed.

"Oh fuck! Oh fuck! Fuck, fuck, fuck!" Skyla cries out around my cock as Ronan growls out his release inside her.

The instant they come down from their high, I'm pushing Ronan to the side and taking his place. Skyla turns around to face me, her soft skin gently moving against mine. One of my hands comes to her hip, the other moving to her growing belly as I push inside her.

"There you are," I whisper.

She smiles at me, forcing my heart to clench in my chest as she rolls her hips in slow, fluid motions. My eyes roll to the back of my head as I hear the others.

"Don't pout. I'll suck you off, Ash," Liam says.

"And I'll take care of this tight ass while you do," Wesley says before climbing behind Liam and pushing inside him.

Liam arches his back and moans as Asher shoves himself down Liam's throat. I never know who's fucking who with those four. Well, obviously the only two that don't are Asher and Ronan, but still. Asher always acts like he only loves Liam, but I catch him and Wesley fucking just as much. Then Ronan will refuse up and down that he loves Wesley, but the jealousy in his eyes currently tells me that's a load of shit.

As if to prove my point, Ronan climbs behind Wesley and begins peppering his back with kisses before pushing a finger inside Wesley's ass and whispering into his ear.

Thank fuck we got a custom bed made for the six of us, otherwise none of this would ever be possible. At least not without being literally all intertwined, and if we can avoid that, I prefer to.

I move my attention back to my siren, and the rest of the world fades. My only focus is her. We don't speak; we don't need to. Our bodies come together as one, and everything else comes second. Being with her is like breathing, like existing. Everything is so... easy.

I feel her walls begin to pulse around me, and her body starts to shudder. She's on the brink of another orgasm already, and I grab her face, forcing her down as far as she can come before my mouth meets hers in the middle.

The instant our lips touch, she falls apart. Her pussy squeezes against me, her body rolling in a way that forcefully steals the cum right out of my cock. It's all hers, though, every fucking drop, and she takes it like a goddamn queen.

When our orgasms fade, she collapses into my arms, and I tuck her carefully into my side, pressing a kiss to the side of her head as the others continue moaning and raw fucking the shit out of each other. I don't care in the slightest, though, as I look down at my entire life.

She's the center of my universe, my entire reason for existence. I understand the fear the Graves brothers feel because if my world was in danger, I'd stop at nothing to protect it, to protect her. My only fear is that my life has brought potential death to those I treasure most. There's only one option, though: we cannot fail. I won't allow it.

Chapter Eight
Zayden

I can't help but press my ear against the wall separating us from the orgy going on next door. My grin widens when I hear one say, "I'll suck you off, Ash."

I laugh. "Oh shit, now the brother husbands are fucking each other!"

"Zayden!" Blake hisses. "Get away from the wall and mind your own goddamn business."

I trot away, bouncing onto the bed beside her. "Oh come on—it's like free porn!"

She shakes her head but can't fight her smile. "You're ridiculous."

"Who is?" Dominic asks as he comes out of the bathroom, a towel wrapped around his waist from his shower.

"Zayden," she answers. "He's eavesdropping on Skyla and her husbands."

"I mean, there are a lot of them. It's hard not to be... curious," Dominic says with a shrug before pulling out his phone. He scrolls through it for a moment before pulling up the hidden nanny cam he placed in the kids' bedroom earlier.

"You put that lock we gave you on the door, right?" Dominic asks as he watches our boys sleep.

"The one that's biometric and a bitch to get on right? Yes," Blake huffs.

Dominic nods, setting his phone down and pressing a kiss to the top of Blake's head. She thinks we're being over the top, but we don't know these people. All we know is that they now have as much to lose as we do, which makes us equal. For now. The idea of leaving Blake and the boys here is like a thousand knives pricking beneath my skin. The alternative, though... There is no alternative. It's our only option, and I know Dominic just fucking hates it.

"I seriously don't think Skyla or the guys would want to hurt the boys. I mean, they're probably worried about us doing the same to their kids."

"As they should be," I say without hesitation.

It's true. If they even breathe wrong on any of my family, I'll split each of their kids stem to stern without a moment's notice.

"Zayden," she admonishes as I shake my head.

"No, angel, you don't get to go soft and drop your guard. We can't leave you here if you're going to let your guard down around these people."

Dominic nods. "He's right, baby. We trust no one else, ever."

"I know, I know. I don't trust them. I just... They seem to get it, or she does, I guess."

"Get what?" Dominic asks.

"This life we live, with kids, having multiple husbands. I don't know. It feels good to be somewhere and not have to... hide."

I frown at that, the loneliness in her words practically echoing in the room. My angel is lonely? How could she be when she has me? And Dominic? And the boys? We would fill our house with even more kids, so she'd never be lonely a day in her life if she'd only let us.

Dominic opens his mouth to get to the bottom of this because that's really what he does best. He's the feelings guy, the understanding one, and I'm an action man. Once direction is given, I run with it. I just need her to tell me how to fix it and I will.

Before Dominic can speak, though, Blake presses a finger to his lips and shakes her head. "I'm fine. The kids are fine. We're all fine. That's what matters."

I nod, and we sit there in silence for a moment before a few moans and groans come through the walls. Jesus, it's a miracle they don't wake up the kids with their sex-a-thon. Then again, maybe that's why all the kids' rooms are on the other side of the house.

As one, we all bust out laughing before I turn my angel's head to me.

"Should we give them a show?"

She grins at me before Dominic nods.

"Let's."

My mouth moves to hers, and our tongues tangle together before Dominic steals her and smashes his lips to hers. A spark of jealousy rips through me as I push him away, stealing her back once more. Dominic scoffs but allows it, as per usual, then I lie on my back, pulling my angel on top of me. He slowly begins undressing her for me, covering her skin with kisses as my hands roam over her body.

Fucking perfection.

When her pants and panties are off, cast to the side, I don't waste a moment before shoving inside her. She moans as Dominic lines himself up behind her. There's the sound of a lube bottle opening and closing, then she tenses around me as he pushes into her ass.

Rule number one of travel with one wife and two husbands: never forget the lube.

"Fuck," she hisses. "I love being full of you both."

"Just the way we like you, baby," Dominic says as he grabs the base of her hair and pulls, forcing her head up.

Another moan sounds from behind us, and Dominic curses.

"Jesus, it sounds like someone is getting full in there too."

"I bet," my angel scoffs in a way that almost sounds like envy.

I push down my jealous rage as an idea flickers in my mind.

I reach into my pocket and pull out my knife with the smooth crystal handle. My angel got it for me as a birthday present last year, but given how often I use it on her, it's practically a gift for her.

"Want to know what it's like? To be stuffed full in your cunt and your ass?" I ask as I press the handle against my cock, right against her entrance.

Her eyes go wide with shock as Dominic's thrusts slow.

"What? I can't take two in my pussy, Zay."

"Sure you can. Open up, angel—I'm coming in."

Before she can protest further, I'm pushing the handle of the knife inside her. The long handle provides me a generous amount of leverage before I have to grip the knife's blade. It pushes against me uncomfortably at first, but then my angel's mouth drops open, and her eyes roll back into her head, and I couldn't stop if I tried.

Her pleasure is like a drug to me, and once I get just a taste, I crave more and more until I'm fucking drowning in it.

"Fuck her ass nice and raw, brother. I'm gonna stuff our wife full."

"Fuck," Dominic curses under his breath as he picks up his pace, helping move her for me as I push more and more of the handle into her. The sharp bite of the blade cuts into my hand, and I feel the first drop of blood hit my skin. The sting is a welcome feeling, one I crave.

When she opens up even further, I begin thrusting in and out of her, keeping the knife in rhythm with me as my beautiful angel turns into a wanton mess on top of me.

"Fuck yes. Let me stretch you, angel. Let's see how much you can take," I say through clenched teeth, my cock already throbbing in her, desperate to come. Not yet, though.

"Oh my God! S-so fu-full," she stutters.

My cock jerks at her words, at her soft moans and whimpers. She's on birth control, despite my irritation. It's what she needs, and I know that, but it won't stop me from speaking my mind.

"Come on my cock, angel. Come all over my knife. I want to smell and taste you while I'm away."

"Zay! Dom!" she moans.

"That's it, baby. Come for us," he says with a sharp slap to her ass that has her bucking.

The knife digs deeper into my palm as more blood spills. My hips are thrusting savagely at this point, words pouring out of my mouth.

"Just like that. I'm gonna come so fucking deep you'll have no choice in giving us another baby. Fuck you nice and pregnant the way you deserve," I say through clenched teeth, though I see the instant my words register.

My angel freezes for a moment, and Dominic casts me an irritated glare. It's not like he doesn't think the same when he's in her cunt. We want more kids desperately. She does too; I know it. She just needs to let go. I'll take care of everything.

Her gaze flickers between the both of us before her orgasm tears through her, seemingly out of nowhere. She moans and shouts to the point Dominic has to cover her mouth as her cunt squeezes the fuck out of me and the knife. My own orgasm washes over me, and I fill her with my cum; Dominic follows right behind, and we both pump her full.

Once the pleasure has passed and Dominic pulls out of her, I can't help but give her a few more thrusts, pushing my cum deeper and deeper, like if I do, it'll break down her birth control and she'll have no choice but to carry my babies.

Slowly, she pushes off me and the knife handle until she's lying on her back beside me. Looking down, she sees the bloody mess my hand has become and absentmindedly drags her finger against my palm, coating the tip of it with blood before she rubs it against her lip. Just like that, I'm hard as a steel pipe once more, and I smash our mouths together. No one gets me like her; no one understands that craving for the pain, for the blood. Not like she does. She's the missing piece to the fucked-up puzzle that is Dominic and me.

"Clean up that fucking hand. We have work to do in a few hours," Dominic says, forcing me to pull away from my angel.

I glower at him but stand, moving to the bathroom to do as he says. He's right. Fucker.

"Hours?" my angel asks as she looks to my brother.

He presses a soft kiss to her lips as he tucks her into him and nods. "We know where one of the Horsemen is, at least now. We can't waste too much time."

"But Grandpa over here needs to rest!" I call out.

"We both need rest. We've been going nonstop for over thirty hours, Zay," he calls back.

Tomato, tomahtoe.

Once my hand is rinsed off, I find some gauze and wrap it for now, then come back to bed and slip in beside my angel. Dominic and I hold her tightly, and I almost think she's asleep until she speaks.

"Are you okay? I mean, I know that sounds like a dumb question in the grand scheme of things, but you seem off... You're not like yourself. This isn't the first time we've experienced something like this, and you've always remained... you."

I'm not sure how to answer her because at this moment, I can't tell what she wants to hear. I'd rather give her whatever lie she needs to hear than what I really feel. Her eyes are pleading for the truth, though, so despite my better judgment, I speak.

"It's my fault," I rasp. "That this is happening to us, that the boys were in danger, that you were. That little Putnam fuck is right, and I hate it."

She frowns, reaching out and cupping my cheek with her hand. "What did he say?"

I shake my head. "Doesn't matter. I just... I need to fix this, as fast as possible. We never rely on people. It's always been just us, and the idea of leaving you with these... people. It's not sitting right with me."

Silence hangs between us for several moments as we stare at each other, the soft pad of her thumb gently moving in circles against my cheek.

"Don't worry about us. I can't describe it, but they feel... safe, at least for now. I'm more worried about you two. Usually, when you have a job, I'm not worried. Not for a second, but now..."

Her words hang in the air like a loaded gun, waiting to go off. Frustration twists in me that she's worried at all. I hate it. I hate it more than anything in the goddamn world. She doesn't deserve to feel worry a moment in her life. Not when she has me. And Dominic too.

I don't reassure her, though, and neither does my brother. I think because for the first time in so long, we're worried too.

Chapter Nine
Asher

I wake up upside down at the foot of the bed, somehow the only one who isn't holding or touching Skyla. What the fuck?

A soft cry sounds through the baby monitor in Brooks's room, and of course none of the other fuckers wake up. Except Sky. Her eyes gently open like she's a princess coming out of a deep sleep. Climbing out of bed, I shake my head at her, then press a kiss to her forehead.

"I've got him, princess," I say.

She gives me a soft smile and a nod before relaxing back into the bed. Such a fucking princess, but she's my princess.

I move to the dresser, grab a pair of sweats out and decide to hell with a shirt as I make my way to Brooks's room. As I'm rubbing my eyes, I find him crying in his bed. He gets these terrible nightmares, and we can't figure out why. We've taken him to the doctor, and even a psychologist at Ronan's insistence, which I thought was a little much since he's only two. Still, this seems to be a weekly occurrence for him, hence why we still have the baby monitor set up for him.

"Hey, bud," I say as I softly shake him awake.

His crying softens as he looks up at me. "Bad dream, Daddy."

I nod. "Do you want to try to go back to sleep?"

He shakes his head. "Cartoons."

I can't help but let a dry laugh out at that. Cartoons it is, then.

I lift him into my arms, letting out a yawn as I walk towards the living room. I grab the remote off the kitchen island and press a button. The light from the TV illuminates the living room and the body sitting on the couch.

"Jesus!" I snap, my heart pounding with adrenaline. It takes a moment for my eyes to adjust, then I see that it's Blake sitting on the couch.

She turns to face me, an apologetic half-smile on her face as she speaks. "Sorry. I didn't think anyone would be up this early."

"Nightmare," I say as I lift Brooks a little higher on my hip.

Blake nods like she knows the feeling all too well before she goes back to staring at the wall.

"Cartoon! Cartoon!" Brooks says, snagging my attention. I quickly put on his favorite show and walk over to the couch.

Brooks takes a seat front and center while Blake sits off to the right and I sit to the left. He's quickly engrossed in his show, and I sit there for a few moments before speaking.

"Sounds like your guys will be leaving soon."

She doesn't respond for a moment, then she nods.

"Vincent is going with them too, to help or whatever. He's good. You shouldn't worry."

Blake's head slowly turns to me, and now I'm able to fully see the haunted look in her eyes. The fear. The pain. Like she too knows nightmares, perhaps greater than any of us. Or maybe she's living her worst one now. "Dom and Zay are too. They're the best, and it still might not be enough to bring them home safe."

I don't have any comforting words, nor do I try to offer any because she's right. From the light research Dominic did last night, these Four Horsemen dudes seem like nothing to fuck with.

Vincent talked about Zayden Graves like he was the Grim Reaper himself, and the way Zayden Graves talks about the Four Horsemen... yeah, I see why she's concerned.

We stay quiet for half the episode before she speaks again.

"You're the group's leader, aren't you?"

I can't help but scoff. Not sure how I feel about being the group's leader. Also not sure how I feel about my marriage being referred to as a group. I do lead the Brethren. I oversee dozens of businesses that are incorporated into our society, but...

"Not really. If anything, Skyla is the leader. We're all happy to exist in her world."

A soft chuckle escapes her as she nods. "That's how the guys talk about me too. The world doesn't normally look at relationships like ours with fondness, but it's nice to meet other people who—"

"Don't give a fuck what anyone else thinks?" I fill in.

She nods. "Exactly."

Another heavy silence passes between us before she turns to face me fully.

"So, no one will tell me what you all actually do. I assume you're not a mercenary like Griggs."

"Definitely not," I scoff. "We're members of a... group. A community."

"Like a cult?" Blake asks.

"No," I snap defensively. "A... society."

"Like a secret one?"

I give her a flat look before lifting an eyebrow. "If I answered that question, it wouldn't be much of a secret, would it?"

She lifts her hands in surrender. "Fair enough. I thought my family lived the most mysterious lifestyle, but this place..." she says as she looks around the cabin. "I think you have us beat."

I shrug as I look down to see Brooks is now passed out, his head on my lap and a small puddle of drool forming on my sweats.

A creak from the other side of the room has me turning my

head to find Zayden, Dominic and Vincent, dressed in all black like they've decided to play spies. Both of the Graves brothers are staring at me with murderous rage.

"Asher, where the fuck are your clothes?" Vincent asks.

I look at him like an idiot because what kind of stupid fucking question is that? Until I look down to see that Brooks is more in my lap than I thought, and from their angle, they probably can't see anything below my bare chest. Quickly, I scooch Brooks off my lap and jump to my feet, holding my hands in the air so one of these psycho fucks doesn't shoot me dead in my own house.

"Brooks was crying, so I got him up, and she was out here."

Blake turns to face them, looking at the knife in Zayden's hand that I'm only now seeing.

"Drop it," she says, much like how you would tell a dog to drop something he shouldn't have.

Zayden doesn't look at her; his eyes are set on mine. Are they nuts? They think that I want their wife? When I have my own and a boyfriend I'm also in love with?

To be fair, I guess if the roles were reversed, someone would already have a bullet hole in their head. Still, all these murder plots are putting everyone on edge and a little too stabby for my taste.

"Zayden," Blake says once more in that same tone.

It's like just his name on her lips is enough to shake him from whatever darkness had captured him. He drops the knife to the floor dramatically, looking to her as if he's awaiting his next instruction.

"We're heading out. Expect us back tonight at the latest," Dominic says.

Blake nods. "We'll be okay. You two stay safe."

She stands and slides an arm around each of their necks. They both wrap their arms around her as she murmurs something to them. They speak to her as well, but I don't attempt to eavesdrop as I walk towards Vincent.

"You good?" I ask.

He nods.

"Are you sure you don't want any backup? Just in case?" I ask as my eyes drift to the Graves brothers, still more than wary of their intentions.

Vincent shrugs. "It's just a job. In and out."

"Okay." I clap my hand on his shoulder. "Stay safe. Skyla barely survived your last death."

Vincent scoffs, shaking his head before nodding as he heads out the door, the Graves twins following closely behind.

Chapter Ten
Skyla

When I woke up this morning, Vincent was gone. My stomach has been twisted into knots since the moment he left, and I don't foresee that fading anytime soon. The guys are extra doting when he's gone—they know how much his work terrifies me. If my stomach is in knots, though, Blake looks like hers is filled with nothing but lead.

The kids wanted to play outside, so Wesley and Ronan did a sweep through the property before letting us all go play out back. I'm sure all of this would seem so odd to others who don't live the lives we do. When you're married to the head of a powerful secret society and nearly all the Elder members in that society... this is just a typical Tuesday.

Blake is walking numbly through the snow after her boys, her eyes vacant as she no doubt thinks and overthinks. I have a lot to be grateful for—that I have some of my husbands here with me to stay by my side. Both of Blake's are gone and she has to pretend to be strong for her boys' sakes in the meantime.

Quickening my pace, I leave Asher and Liam's side to come up beside Blake. Before she can stop me, I slip my arm through hers, looping us together as we continue walking. She looks at me in confusion, but when I smile at her, she returns a smaller one before facing forward.

"They'll be okay," I say.

She nods. "They always are."

Her words agree, but there's still something off about her tone. I watch as her other hand subconsciously touches her stomach, and before I can stop myself, my inner thoughts come blurting out.

"Do they know yet?"

"Know?" she asks.

We stop in our tracks, and I stare at her before my eyes move down to her belly. For a moment, she looks as if she's going to deny what I've known for a little while now. It's not like I really know this woman; maybe it's just intuition or a lucky guess. Regardless, the defeat that enters her eyes as she shakes her head is confirmation enough.

"No."

I nod as we continue walking once more, watching as Liam takes off running for the kids, throwing snowballs at them like the giant child he is.

"Are you thinking about getting an abor—?"

"No," she snaps quickly. "No."

I should probably drop it. She clearly doesn't want to talk about this, yet for some reason, I can't help but pry. Maybe it's helping keep my mind off things right now, or maybe I'm just a nosey bitch.

"I struggled," she says first. "With the twins. The pregnancy was great, the birth was fine... as fine as birth can be."

I laugh at that and nod as she continues.

"It was after. The days... they got so dark. So cold. I don't know if it was sleep deprivation, stress or something wrong with me. I wasn't... right. I don't want to feel like that again. Ever," she says, her eyes meeting mine, shimmering with unshed tears.

My heart aches for her as Seraphina and the twins run up to us.

"Mommy! I want to bake cookies!"

I nod and smile at her. "Later, baby."

"Okay! Tag!" she says, tagging one of the boys before she takes off running.

I turn back to Blake to see all emotion wiped from her face, like she's put it away into a tiny box, never to see the light of day again.

I pull off one of my snow gloves, do the same for Blake and intertwine our fingers as I speak. "I personally haven't suffered post birth like you have, so I won't offer you glittering words and false promises. What I can tell you, though, is your husbands seem to be ready to burn the world down for your family. They clearly love you and the boys more than life itself. I know they want to do anything to help you through anything. Whatever you need, it seems that they'd be willing to give you anything without a second of hesitation."

Blake blinks at that and nods, choosing not to speak as I continue.

"I know it's not easy to ask for help in those moments. I know sometimes you probably won't even know what to ask for, but I can tell they're the type of men that won't stop until you're taken care of the way you need to be."

"They've both wanted more kids for so long now. I've been the one standing in the way, and when my period was late... I was terrified. I was scared. Isn't that disgusting? That for a moment, for more than just one moment, honestly, I was upset about my growing child?" Blake asks.

"You went through the darkness and came out the other side, Blake. That was your experience. No one else's. If you don't think you can do it again, then you need to express that and protect your peace and family. If you want to try, then let your husbands sit with some of that heaviness. Lord knows we didn't marry multiple men for the sex; it's guaranteed princess treatment for life."

Blake laughs at that as she watches the boys play.

"This all seems inconsequential with a group of mercenaries trying to kill my family. Who knows, maybe none of us will live long enough to even worry about it?"

Her dark humor is clearly a deflection tactic, but I can't help the chuckle that rips through me.

"That's the spirit."

Chapter Eleven
Liam

"I want the green sprinkles!" Jackson snaps at Brooks, who's currently hogging the highly sought-after green Christmas tree sprinkles.

"Mine!" Brooks shouts, slapping Jackson in the face.

Jackson then turns to Skyla with his mouth wide open and the most desperate-sounding cry. She comes to him instantly, shushing him as Asher picks Brooks up.

"Not cool, little man. You know we don't hit."

I hear Brooks argue with Ash as he carries him down the hall to his room. Ronan went to pick up dinner for all of us, and Wesley is currently helping Ryder, Seraphina and Aries decorate cookies.

Once Skyla has calmed Jackson down, he jumps to the floor and pulls on Aries.

"C'mon—let's go play!"

Aries looks back at Seraphina and Ryder, who seem perfectly content decorating. When Seraphina looks up, though, her eyes lock on Aries, and she turns to Ryder.

"We can make more later."

Ryder nods, and the four of them run off together towards the playroom.

"Shit. Jackson! Come back here and wipe your hands, you fucking animal!" Wesley says as he jogs after him.

Skyla sighs, shaking her head as she calls out, "Language, Wes."

She begins moving the cookie mess to the other counter, clearing off the kitchen island as I come up behind her. I wrap my arms around her waist, resting my hands on her belly as I smile into her neck.

"We both know these kids will be raised by the foulest mouths. Why fight it?"

She huffs out an irritated breath as she looks over her shoulder at me. "Because it's inappropriate."

I scoff at that, pressing soft kisses to her neck the way I do whenever I want to get out of trouble with her. Works like a charm.

"Liam," she grumbles while angling her neck for more kisses.

"Yeah, babygirl?"

"The kitchen is a mess, and we have company."

My eyes pop open, and I lock gazes with Blake, who's watching us with a knowing smirk.

"Our company doesn't seem to mind. She knows the drill: make out when you can, where you can, right?"

Blake nods, lifting her cup of hot chocolate. "Hear, hear."

"There ya go," I say as I spin Skyla around, then sink my fingers into the back of her hair to hold her closer as my lips press to hers.

She's unyielding only for a moment before she softens in my arms, her tongue twirling around my own. I moan into her mouth. Fuck, I've been craving this. I love sex, all kinds of sex really, but sometimes nothing beats a good make-out sesh.

My hands move to her thighs before I'm lifting her into the air and onto the kitchen island. Stepping in between her legs, my hands begin to drift when a voice speaks from over my shoulder, scaring the living shit out of me.

"What the fuck do you think you're doing?"

I yelp, spinning around to see Zayden Graves staring at me with a scowl. Blake moves from her seat, practically throwing herself into his arms. He catches her easily, his gaze never wavering from me as his scowl deepens.

"Did you just fucking screech? Did he screech, angel? Is this really one of the men that's supposed to look after my family? A screecher?"

Blake smacks his arm, and I shrug.

"You scared me."

Zayden doesn't look pacified by that, but I don't really give a fuck.

"Any reason you're putting on a fucking porno in front of my wife, Walcott?"

I scoff. "Please, my cock hasn't even come out yet. This was the start of the show. You're just in time," I say with a waggle of my eyebrows.

Zayden shakes his head as his eyes come to Skyla. "Should I fetch one of your other husbands so you can actually be pleased? No doubt the little screecher falls short in that department."

I don't take insults well; they always just feel like challenges to me. And in this case, challenge accepted.

"I can please my wife better than you can please yours—that's a guaran-fucking-tee."

Zayden laughs. "You're out of your mind."

I look at him with a challenging glint. "Prove it."

Zayden watches me carefully before I push on Skyla's chest, forcing her to lie flat on her back.

"Liam," she says.

"Shh, I'm proving a point, babygirl."

When I turn to look at Zayden, he already has Blake lifted onto the counter, her lying down in a similar position as he reaches for her pants.

"You look at what's mine, I'll cut your fucking eyes out," he snarls.

"Trust me, Graves, the only pussy I'm interested in is right in front of me. You, however…" I say with a salacious grin that has him bristling, but it gives me the perfect advantage to slip Skyla's leggings and panties down as I go to work.

My tongue runs through her and she lets out a shocked gasp. I hear a similar one leave Blake in the next moment, but honestly, I'm a little too scared to look and verify. I don't doubt that Zayden is crazy enough to stab me in the goddamn neck just for glancing in their direction, so I focus on my wife and getting her off as many times as possible. Truly, my area of expertise.

I swirl my tongue around her clit, nipping and sucking in a way I've perfected over the years. Sky must have been feeling a little built up because it takes virtually no effort to get her first orgasm. She moans and groans, squirming against the counter. Unfortunately, the victorious feeling that washes over me fades almost instantly when Blake arrives at her first orgasm. Fuck.

I slide a finger inside Skyla, pushing it in and out of her before adding another and another. She gasps and digs her hand into my hair, pushing my face harder against her. Fuck. I love it when she takes control like this. *Wait, no, Liam. Focus.*

I curl my fingers up, rubbing against her G-spot, and her pussy spasms around my fingers. In the next second, the sound of Blake's second orgasm hits the room, and I increase my speed and pressure, causing Skyla to come right along with her.

When Zayden keeps going, Blake practically begs for a break. "Please, Zay. Too much… too fast. I need—"

"One more, angel. Give me one more," he says.

I can't help myself—my eyes move to the side to see Zayden already staring at me, that look of challenge in his eyes, but his mouth holds a slight smirk like he knows he's about to win. His tongue licks through Blake as he winks at me, and goddamnit, my cock throbs because how fucking hot is this? Knowing that Sky needs something more to get off, I pull away, pushing my pants down and palming my cock before lining myself up to her.

"How many fucking piercings do you have?" Zayden practically snarls.

"Not enough," Skyla moans as I sink inside her.

I chuckle as I begin thrusting my hips, victory within reach as Blake and Skyla both begin shaking. I watch them pat around the island, desperately trying to hold on to anything before their hands intertwine. My cock throbs again as I push myself against Sky's G-spot, right on the edge of my own orgasm because how fucking hot is it that I'm fucking my wife as Graves is eating his and our wives are holding hands? That is cutesy shit right there.

I feel Sky about to fall over the edge, and I smirk to Zayden in victory. His eyes meet mine, and the next thing I know, he's pulling a knife out of his pocket, flicking it open and cutting a line against Blake's upper thigh.

"What the fuck?" I yelp as she moans.

My jaw is practically on the floor as he digs his fingers into the cut, playing with her blood as he speaks.

"You bleed too good for me, angel. Come on my tongue while my fingers are painted with you."

Blake begins to tremble before Zayden moves to lick the bleeding cut, his tongue quickly covered in blood. I know Vincent and Skyla have dabbled with knife play, but I've never witnessed it first-hand. I can't lie—it's not for me. This motherfucker is absolutely crazy, and based on how his woman is loving it, she's just as fucking nuts.

Somehow, the bloody little show beside me isn't enough to deter my orgasm, and I moan as Blake and Skyla both fall apart simultaneously. They each writhe and wiggle against the countertop as I wring out every ounce of pleasure I can possibly get before collapsing on top of Skyla.

The room is quiet for a moment before I pull away from Skyla and look at Zayden. He's already watching me, irritation in his expression.

I, however, smirk. "Guess it's a tie."

"I could do this all day," he scoffs.

"Me too, but our girls look like they need a break," I reply as I look at the absolute puddles they've become, chests heaving as they still cling to each other on the kitchen island.

Zayden looks to them, frowning slightly before I speak.

"But you haven't gotten off yet, and I'm available," I say with my most charming smile. "With your wife's permission of course."

Blake looks at me, interest sparking in her eyes as Zayden drives his fist into my stomach. It knocks the wind out of me, though I can't help but laugh.

"Keep your goddamn mouth the fuck away from me."

I smile up at him. "You say that now, but trust me, I give head like no one else."

Zayden shakes his head as he pulls Blake down from the counter, covering her up as I do the same for Skyla. After I stuff my cock back in my pants of course.

"Where's Dom?" Blake asks.

"Right here, baby," he says as he steps through the door alongside Vincent.

Skyla practically shoves me out of the way and runs to Vincent. He holds her tight, burying his head into her hair as he begins speaking softly. I run a hand through my own hair as Dominic hugs Blake before he looks between Zayden and me.

"What did we miss?"

Zayden and I look at each other. There's a smile playing on his lips that mirrors my own. Then we both shake our heads.

"Nothing," we say together.

Dominic looks at us for a second longer, like he doesn't believe us, before the door opens once more.

Ronan steps through with bags upon bags of takeout. "I'm home! Who's hungry?" he calls out.

"Not me; I'm stuffed," I say with a smirk.

Zayden looks to me with a smirk. "Me too. Couldn't eat another bite."

I cackle at that, clapping him on the shoulder. When he's not being all uptight and slasher-killer-like, I really dig this crazy fucker.

Chapter Twelve
Vincent

Our search for Augustus came up short yesterday. We scoured the streets of Buffalo from top to bottom and came up empty, though Zayden was finally able to track down a nice little rat that could tell us where Augustus's newest home was.

That's what's brought us to Chicago. An ostentatious mansion that would fit in well in Salem lies before us, all lights off as the residents get some much-needed rest. While they can.

Dominic was able to hack into the security feed and loop it so we could slip in and out. He was also able to confirm that our target is passed out in bed with a few women, no doubt prostitutes because I don't think anyone would willingly sleep with the ugly piece of shit.

Thanks to Dominic, we literally walk through the front door. The cocky asshole didn't even lock his fucking door. All three of us move our heads like they're on a swivel as we assess the situation, ready for anything as we slowly creep up the grand staircase.

Zayden is the first to push through the door, followed by myself and Dominic. I can feel their distrust in me still, and I don't blame them. I don't exactly trust them either. It's not in our nature to work as a team on anything. Well, maybe them, but they're the exception. In our line of work, it's kill or be killed, and the way you avoid being killed is by being the quickest and the fastest. Neither of those occur within a team too well, typically.

Just as Dominic's surveillance told us, Augustus Popov is passed out in the middle of the bed, a naked woman on either side of him. One of them even has a needle still hanging from her arm. Lovely.

I see Zayden's intent as he creeps towards the closest woman, his knife drawn, but I shake my head as I touch his arm. He frowns, questioning why I would cut into his playtime as I move closer to the bed. I'll do whatever it takes to complete a job, but I don't take pleasure in the kill the way Zayden does. I enjoy completing a mission, eradicating filth from this earth. Women, though? Women I don't enjoy killing.

Okay, well, I did enjoy killing Annie Williams, but that girl was a nasty cunt, and she was trying to break my siren's heart by forcing herself onto Ronan, so in that matter, it was a great pleasure. Regardless, these women aren't the focus of our mission for the night, and the quicker we complete this, the quicker I can get home to my siren. Fuck knows what the others are up to with her.

I feel Zayden's and Dominic's eyes on me as I lean over one of the women to reach Augustus, carefully covering his mouth with my gloved hand before jamming my knife into his carotid. His eyes fly open as my blade sinks into his flesh, his grunts and groans muffled behind my hand as I twist the knife ninety degrees before sinking it in further. He attempts to buck against me before the fight slowly leeches out of him and his eyes go vacant. I twist the knife once more for good measure before ripping it out, essentially tearing his neck to shreds.

Blood pours from him by the liter, staining the crisp white sheets to a deep red. The unconscious women are soon surrounded by his blood, like they're swimming in a crimson lake.

"Nicely done, Griggs," Zayden says with a smile, a laugh begging to slip through his words as he holds his hand out, awaiting a high five or some shit.

He doesn't whisper; in fact, I think he speaks loud enough to wake the girls on purpose. Their eyes flutter open, dazed and confused, before Zayden snaps one of their necks with a sharp crack while Dominic pulls out a gun and shoots the other between the eyes. Their swift actions take me by surprise and I stare at them.

"No loose ends, Griggs. We aren't playing for fun—this is about our family," Dominic says with a shrug before he turns and walks out into the hallway.

Zayden nods as he rifles through the room, pocketing Augustus's phone and wallet. "Yeah! No loose ends, Griggsy. Plus, we can't let you have all the fun. This is *our* revenge," Zayden says in a teasing way that has me shaking my head.

Griggsy? I swear to God if Liam hears him call me that, it will become his entire personality, and then I'll have to kill him, and Skyla will be seriously pissed with me.

Shaking my head, I follow after them, and we exit the mansion, heading for the car parked down the road. None of us speak until we're inside the car. I climb into the driver's seat and head for the cabin.

"One down, three to go," Dominic murmurs, more to himself than anyone as his fingers begin flying across his phone screen.

"Who are we going after next, Dom?" Zayden asks as I merge onto the highway.

"You already know Desmond and Dennis will be holed up together until it suits them," Dominic responds.

"Why is that?" I ask.

"Because Dennis doesn't have two brain cells to rub together, and Desmond believes in family too much to let him fuck off and die," Zayden says.

I nod. "So Andre, then?"

Dominic nods. "Yeah. We need to gather intel on him fast. As soon as the others discover Augustus is dead, they'll go underground until they can counterattack."

I frown at that and look at him in the rearview mirror. "Counterattack? I don't like the sound of that."

"Neither do we. Why do you think we came knocking on your door?" Zayden asks. "We can handle the Four Horsemen in a one-on-one fight, but their resources... the amount of men they have at their disposal. We wouldn't live long enough to take them all out."

Dominic points to his brother in agreement, not taking his eyes off the phone as he continues his work.

I knew allowing them into our home was going to be a dangerous thing, but I don't think I fully grasped how bad things could get. Suddenly, a million plans and ideas are running through my head. Maybe I need to get Skyla and the kids out of the country for a while. Europe maybe? Australia? Fuck, I don't know, but the safeguards of our winter cabin suddenly aren't filling me with much confidence.

"What do you need access to?" I ask.

"Just about anything your brother husbands can get their hands on," Zayden says as he flicks open his knife, examining the blood that stains the metal like it's the most fascinating thing in the world.

"Will you stop fucking calling them that?" I grit through clenched teeth.

Zayden's eyes move to mine, a taunting smirk on his lips as he speaks.

"No."

Chapter Thirteen
Blake

Skyla already has a decorated Christmas tree with more presents than you would think could possibly fit beneath one, but after an incident with Liam, Wesley and my boys involving a football inside the house... let's just say there were a few casualties among the glass ornaments. I cringed when I saw the beautiful tree flat on the floor, covering dozens of expensive-looking presents, mentally calculating how much each damaged item would cost. Don't get me wrong, the boys and I are completely comfortable. We have more than we could ever spend in this life or the next. These people, though... they're next-level rich, and it shows.

The guys claimed the blame, though I knew my boys were behind the incident based on their guilty faces, and Skyla all but shrugged it off before turning to me.

"I've been wanting to get a few last-minute presents anyways, and Vincent finally isn't around, so it's the perfect time to get him something. Besides, you guys might be with us through the holiday, and the boys don't have anything under the tree."

True. All their presents were left at the safe house in the Caribbean; they just didn't seem like a priority when we were packing up. Logically, they still aren't, but I don't want Aries or Ryder to wake up on Christmas with nothing for them.

"C'mon—the mall is only a thirty-minute drive, and it's not too bad for in-store selections," she says.

I hesitate, looking around as if Dominic and Zayden can hear us. "I don't know. My husbands were very clear that me and the boys shouldn't leave the house."

She laughs lightly. "Blake, we essentially have a private protection detail with my husbands alone. And Asher and Liam can stay at home and manage the kids."

Uncertainty flickers inside me. I'm not sure how I feel about leaving the boys behind, even if it's only for a few hours. When I look to Skyla, though, I see no malice in her gaze; I feel no ill intent. It may seem asinine, but I feel I can trust her, and trust her husbands by extension. Again, probably asinine of me.

"We'll be there and back in no time," she says.

"You'll be where and back?" Wesley asks.

She turns to him and smiles, pressing a soft kiss to his lips that seems to melt him right where he stands. "The mall. You and Ronan will come with us," she says like it's a done deal.

He lifts an eyebrow in curiosity and tilts his head to the side. "Oh yeah? Just like that?"

"Just like that," she says with a smile.

"I don't know, little one. Convincing Ro might be more difficult than you think."

"What will be difficult?" Ronan asks as he strolls into the room.

He wraps his arm around Skyla's waist, effectively stealing her from Wesley, and places a kiss to her lips. Wesley doesn't seem to mind one bit; in fact, he seems to be downright enjoying himself as their kiss lingers.

When they pull away, Skyla intertwines her arms around his neck, batting her eyes at him as she softens her voice. "Daddy."

"Oh Christ," he mutters, tilting his head to the sky like he's not ready for whatever she's about to ask.

When he looks back down at her, even I can see that she's got him in the palm of her hand. She smiles at him sweetly as she speaks, while he seems to hang on her every word.

"Blake and I want to go to the mall to get the boys some Christmas presents. And I haven't bought anything for Vincent yet. It's the perfect opportunity."

Ronan winces like he's struggling against her womanly wiles— at least that's what I assume is going on in his inner monologue.

"Baby, that's not a good idea. Why can't you buy some things online?"

"There's no guarantee what we want will get here before Christmas, and we've been cooped up for too long."

He gives her a flat look as he lifts an eyebrow. "It's been a few days."

"Semantics," she says with a wave of her hand. "Please, Daddy. Pleeeease."

Skyla begins kissing Ronan's neck, and I watch as his resolve evaporates almost immediately. His eyes close, and he nods, tightening his grip on her as he responds.

"Fine, but Wesley and I will be sticking to the two of you like glue."

Skyla pulls away, an excited little bounce to her step as she nods. "Wouldn't have it any other way. Let me just go get changed," she says and practically waddles up the stairs with her cute little baby bump to her room.

Ronan turns to me with an assessing gaze. "How likely is it that one of your husbands will skin me alive if they find out I let you out of this place?"

"Ten out of ten, though Dom much prefers to shoot his kills, so maybe nine out of ten if he can beat Zay to it."

He scoffs, running a hand through his hair as Wesley laughs.

"Well, goddamn. Gotta love those odds, huh, Ro?"

"Yeah, fucking great," he snarks back.

Twenty minutes later, Skyla came out of her bedroom, alongside Asher and Liam, who both were rocking just-had-sex hair. All of their cheeks were flushed, and their foreheads were dotted with sweat. Fuck, I know having five husbands must mean a lot of sex, but this girl has to be the horniest woman who's ever lived. I kinda love it for her, though.

Wesley climbed into the driver's seat as Ronan sat up front, and Skyla and I took the back of the blacked-out SUV. We all chatted lightly at first before the conversation casually quieted.

Now, I find myself practically mesmerized by the white streets. It reminds me so much of Chicago. I didn't realize how much I loved living in a snow-covered city with nearly guaranteed white Christmases until I moved to Seattle. Just cold enough to be miserable, just warm enough to only rain. Sometimes we get the occasional flurry that quickly melts away, but nothing like out here.

Skyla snickers beside me, and I look to see her texting on her phone. Her eyes catch mine, and she smirks before showing me the screen.

"This is my best friend Maggie's daughter. She's three now and apparently did a whole presentation at preschool about why having two mommies is better than one."

I look down at the beautiful redheaded little girl. She looks like that princess with the crazy flowing hair and bright green eyes.

I laugh. "I mean, cleaner house, less noise. I see her point."

Skyla nods along, typing out a reply to her friend.

"How long have you been friends?" I ask.

"Gosh, almost seven years or something, right?" she asks the guys.

"With Maggie. With Bridgette... less," Ronan says as he and Wesley chuckle.

I tilt my head in curiosity as Skyla rolls her eyes before looking to me.

"Bridgette and I have a little history. Once upon a time, she was in love with Asher and did not want me at her school. We were in college, but once she and Maggie fell in love, all was well."

Wesley snickers. "Kinda."

"Enough," Skyla scoffs with a laugh. "Bridgette is a little... high maintenance. Maggie loves her to pieces, but I swear to God I thought she was going to kill her while she was pregnant. They used Maggie's egg and a donor, and then Bridgette carried their baby, but my God, that was nine months of hell for everyone within a five-mile radius."

I laugh at that, feeling blessed that my pregnancy with the boys was decently easy.

The reminder of my current... condition has a fearful feeling sinking into my stomach. I know I have to tell Zayden and Dominic soon. They both track my period, like psychos. I'm already two weeks late. I think the only reason they haven't put it together yet is because of this whole mess we're in.

Skyla chuckles once more before pocketing her phone. I smile at her, though I can't help but feel a little envious. It must be nice to have tight-knit friends, or a tight-knit friend and her wife that you tolerate. I really just have... the guys and the twins. I'm not saying I don't love my family or my life because I do, so much. I guess I never slowed down long enough to realize that I really don't have anything outside of them. Maybe that's what terrifies me about this pregnancy, or maybe that's why my first postpartum experience was so dark. I had nothing but... this, and it was too easy to get lost in the chaos of it all.

"You okay?" Skyla asks, resting her hand on mine in sympathy.

I do my best to smile. "Yeah, I just... I don't really have any friends. Kinda jealous of you." I laugh lightly. "I had one friend growing up, and she turned out to be a fucking cunt," I say.

Skyla frowns at that before nodding. "Before Maggie, I really didn't have any friends either. Acquaintances but never anyone who got me, you know?"

"Yeah. It's probably really nice to have that."

The car is quiet for a moment before Skyla squeezes my hand. "Well, you've got that now."

I smile at her and squeeze her hand in return. I guess so.

Chapter Fourteen
Wesley

Ronan and I have so many bags in our hands, my arms are starting to hurt. Seriously. Do not let my wife loose in a mall a week before Christmas with her little black credit card unless you're ready to do some serious lifting. Asher's nickname for her is truly accurate. She's a fucking princess, but she's our princess.

We found some cool remote-controlled cars for Aries and Ryder as well as a drone that I'm sure they'll get into nothing but trouble with. Skyla said she needed to find something for Vincent, but honestly the man would love nothing more than a coupon for uninterrupted Skyla time. I think he'd be over the moon for that, and I told her so, to which she rolled her eyes and strolled into a clothing store.

Her fingers dance over cashmere sweaters and silk dress shirts, neither of which come close to Vincent's "style." If ripped black jeans and a leather jacket can be considered style.

"What do you think of this?" she asks me.

I look to Ronan, who's keeping a careful eye on Blake and therefore providing no backup as I shake my head. "Looks great, little one. Can we go now?"

She pouts. "We can go as soon as you help me. Do you think this is too short for him? He's about your height."

"Yeah, but I'm more built," I say with a flex of my arms.

Skyla sighs, shaking her head as she holds the sweater up to me. "You know, you should really be more cooperative. I spotted a dressing room in the back corner of the store that's unattended."

Now she's fucking talking.

Nothing else needs to be said. In half a second, I drop all the bags to the floor and scoop her up, tossing her over my shoulder as I haul ass to the back of the store. She giggles the whole way, and I even hear a store attendant call out to us before Ronan intervenes.

I step inside the dressing room and shut the door behind me, locking it, then pinning Skyla's hands above her head. My mouth is on hers before she can even breathe, our tongues intertwining. A soft little moan escapes her that has my cock dripping pre-cum already.

"Fuck, little one. I'm so goddamn hard for you."

She smirks against my lips. "Prove it."

I let out a low growl, kicking the velvet-covered bench around so it suits us better before I lay her out across it. Skyla smirks, slowly lifting her ass up so that I can pull her pants down. They're those stretchy maternity pants that come off so easily, which is honestly all of our preference. Before we had kids, there would be days where Skyla would be in absolutely nothing, and it was fucking glorious.

"So do you like the sweater or not? You think Vincent will like it?"

I laugh. "He'll love anything you give him."

I reach down, grabbing the sweater she carried in here before I rub it against her bare thigh. She quivers at the touch before letting out another sweet moan.

"Feel how soft it is, little one. Tell me he won't go crazy over it," I practically purr.

She nods shakily, her hips wiggling as I dance the material against her swollen clit.

"Fuck," she whimpers.

I grin. "You like that?"

"Uh-huh."

I do it again and again before I rest part of the neckline against her clit, covering it with my hand as I start rubbing soft circles. "There you go, little one. Make a mess all over your husband's sweater. It'll be the best present he ever got."

A breathy gasp leaves her, and I decide that I can't take the torture anymore. I push my cock into her, letting out a low groan as I sink fully inside. Her pussy pulses around me as I begin thrusting, rubbing the sweater against her faster. Does anyone know what cum does to cashmere? It has to only enhance it, right? At least, in Vincent's opinion it will.

I thrust in and out of her, desperate to fill her with my release as I rest a hand on her hip, holding her for better leverage. Fuck. I love her like this. Soft, open and fucking drenched for me. The group play we all have is fun, but sometimes a moment like this with my wife is all I need.

"Wes," she pants.

"I know, little one. I know," I say through clenched teeth. "You want my cum? Want me to fill you up?"

"Yes," she moans. "I want your cum, please," she begs.

I can't help but chuckle. It's no wonder she's practically been permanently pregnant since we got married. My wife has the need-iest breeding kink, and so do the rest of us. By the time we're done with her, we're going to have a few hundred kids. Sounds like a good fucking time in the process.

The base of my spine begins to tingle, and my balls tighten before I empty myself inside her. Wave after wave of pleasure crashes over me, and neither Skyla nor myself attempt to conceal our pleasure as we fall apart together. Fuck them, who gives a shit if anyone knows that I can please my wife?

When we come up for air, I lean down, pressing a soft kiss to her lips before pulling myself out. The sweater is still balled up in my fist, and I raise it to my nose, inhaling deeply and groaning because all I can smell is her.

Yeah, Vincent's gonna fucking love it.

I grab another end of the sweater, unable to stop myself from fucking with Vincent at least a little. I use the sweater to clean between Skyla's thighs, and she looks to me in surprise before a laugh escapes her.

When we get to the front, Ronan is watching us with a patient shake of his head, Blake has a surprised shit-eating grin and the saleswoman looks downright mortified.

"Just the sweater, then?" she asks.

"You might want to throw in the shirt that's in the dressing room. Not sure you'll be able to sell it now."

"Jesus," Ronan says from behind us, doing his best to conceal his laugh as I turn around and shoot him a wink.

Skyla hands the woman her card, not an ounce of shame in her smile before she takes her new purchase, and we all head out of the store. The girls link arms and begin whispering and giggling as Ronan steps up beside me, handing me the bags I dropped before clapping my shoulder and whispering into my ear.

"Hope you're ready for round two later. Listening to you two has me hard as a fucking pipe."

Surprise hits me when I see Ronan is watching me with hungry eyes. He usually never approaches me first. It's always the other way round, and typically, it's after a few beers or when we're having one of our weekly—okay, daily—fuckfests. This... this is new, and I definitely don't hate it.

Deciding to tease him a bit, I lower my hand, "accidently" brushing against his leg, and it takes no effort at all to feel his rock-hard cock. Goddamnit. My own cock jerks in anticipation, and I'm suddenly scrambling, thinking of places that we can sneak off to in the middle of this crowded mall.

Ronan wets his lips, and I smile at him when something catches my attention over his shoulder. A man wearing a hat, suspiciously pulled way too low, and holding up his phone in our direction. He doesn't see me because he's too busy taking pictures ahead. Pictures of the girls.

In an instant, Ronan catches on to my change of focus before turning around to see what I've spotted.

"What the fuck?" he says quietly.

The man locks eyes with us for half a second before quickly pocketing his phone and walking in the other direction.

"I'm gonna follow him," I say as I head off in the same direction.

"Wes, wait—"

My eyes meet his for a moment before I see the man has broken into a full sprint. I take off after him, calling out over my shoulder. "Get the girls to the car!"

I dodge other mallgoers, bobbing and weaving between them before I begin throwing people. The guy in front of me is fast, and I don't know if he has others with him or waiting somewhere.

"Stop!" I shout after him.

He turns to look at me over his shoulder before pulling out a gun and firing a round. I jolt to the side, and the bullet narrowly misses me as he takes off for the stairs to the parking garage. I follow him, bursting through the door as a body comes flying towards me. The butt of a gun jams into the side of my eye, forcing me to see stars.

I reach out and quickly wrap the gun in my grasp before the guy headbutts me—not successfully I'll add because he stumbles back, holding his head with a wince.

No one ever wins with a headbutt.

He recovers faster than I do, though, and takes off running once more. I stumble a few steps before chasing after him up the flights of stairs. We pass level after level before he pushes out one door and takes off through the garage. He's over thirty yards away from me, but he's close enough that I have a clean shot, and I take it. My bullet sinks into his calf, and he yells before collapsing.

Suddenly, a car pulls up beside him, and he reaches for the handle. Instead of the door opening, the window rolls down and a gun emerges, two rapid shots hitting him in the head before the car peels out. My head swivels to the black sedan as I shout the license plate out over and over, so I don't forget it.

"AZ41TT3. AZ41TT3. AZ41TT3."

I jog over to the now deceased man and roll him over to see if I can identify him. He doesn't look familiar, though. Not to me anyways.

After pulling out my phone, I see three missed calls from Ronan and two from Skyla. I call Ronan first and am met with his thundering voice.

"WHERE ARE YOU?"

"South parking garage, fifth floor," I heave through labored breaths. "Hurry. We have a body."

The line goes dead, and I pull up the group chat I have with the guys and send a text. I don't know who that was or what they want, but I know they're no friends of ours. I also know that whoever killed him isn't a friend either. More than likely they just wanted to make sure that he couldn't talk if I was able to catch him. He wasn't working alone, which means anyone could have pictures of the girls and their location right now. Maybe even more.

Me: We've got a serious fucking problem.

Chapter Fifteen
Dominic

I'm trying not to lose my fucking shit, but the ability is escaping me.

"What part of *don't leave the fucking house* was confusing?" I spit as I look around the room of clueless idiots.

We were forty-five minutes from the cabin when Vincent's phone buzzed. He glanced at it, and his body went rigid before Zayden grabbed the phone out of his hand and showed it to me.

"What the fuck is that supposed to mean?" I scoffed.

"Nothing good," he muttered before snatching it away from Zayden and calling his wife.

It took a few rings before her shaky voice echoed through the phone.

"Siren, talk to me," he practically begged.

"Some guy was following us at the mall. He got pictures of us. I... I don't know. He's dead now, I guess. We're going to meet Wesley."

"The mall? What the fuck are you doing at the mall? Is my family with you?" Zayden practically snarled.

"Blake is," she said softly.

I closed my eyes, letting out a ragged breath. We stayed on the line the entire time until Wesley and the body were in their vehicle, and we made it to the cabin in twenty minutes. Normally, I fucking hate reckless drivers, but in that moment, Vincent couldn't slam his foot far enough to the floor.

Zayden and Vincent battled to burst through the door first, one going for Wesley while the other went for Ronan. Both got several good hits in on them before they were pried off by the others. I, however, took my time as I stepped into that room. I needed to, or I was going to fucking lose it.

I am composed, I am collected. Not right now, though. Right now, I feel as out of control as I imagine Zayden feels daily. I'm fearful to even touch my wife or children, unsure of what the raging beast inside me will do with all of this... anger.

Clenching my fists by my side, I verbally annihilate everyone in the room until they're dust beneath my feet.

"We asked for your aid, a request that should have been granted without hesitation, yet you all deem it appropriate to put the love of our lives in danger? The mother to our children? Tell me, are you so arrogant that you thought you could stand toe to toe with anyone who dares cross you or so ignorant that you didn't believe us when we warned of very real danger awaiting an opportunity?" I snarl as I look between Ronan and Wesley.

Wesley speaks up, definite shame in his tone. "The girls wanted to get some Christmas presents for your sons. They've been stuck in the house. They just wanted—"

"I don't give a fuck what they wanted! Be reckless with your wife all you want, but if you so much as put a single hair on Blake's head in danger, I will break every goddamn bone in your body with a tiny hammer and then I will fucking kill you!"

Zayden's hand comes to rest on my shoulder, his way of attempting to rein me in, but it's useless. This rage inside me is an all-consuming fiery blaze that I have no way to put out. No desire to either.

"Dom, calm down," Blake says, but I cut her a look so feral, she sinks back into the couch and swallows, looking properly chastised.

"You will not tell me to calm down! You fucking know better! You knew better, goddamnit! You—"

A fist drives into the side of my face, forcing me to the ground. When I blink away the stars, Zayden is grasping my shirt, pressing his nose to my own as he snarls, "Do not swear at my wife! You will apologize. NOW!"

I feel the prick of cold metal and only now register that Zayden has a knife pressed to my neck with his other hand. I'm sure the others are bewildered at the sight before them. Surely, none of them would ever contemplate harming one another. Maybe Griggs, but other than that... Zayden and I... we're different, though. We were raised different; we grew up different. The difference is that I love my brother dearly; he's my other half. He's the only blood family I have, but the truth is the same for both of us. If it came down to our wife and children's protection and our lives, we would both gladly gut the other with little to no remorse.

I look to Blake, struggling to utter a single word of remorse when I feel no such thing. She was careless with her life, careless with our hearts. She knows better. Just because these boys let Skyla prance around like a spoiled princess doesn't mean that our wife doesn't know better. It's not like the five-foot-nothing privileged little girl poses any physical or emotional threat. So I cannot for the life of me understand why my level-headed, rational wife would do something so monumentally stupid.

Slowly, Blake stands and walks towards us before reaching out and touching Zayden's hand. In an instant, he drops the knife, allowing it to clatter against the floor. It's as if Blake's skin against his is Zayden's very own reset button. He completely shuts down for her, becoming wholly subservient to her every desire.

Once Zayden releases me, Blake comes to kneel before me, lowering her head as she speaks.

"I'm sorry."

My temper slowly recedes, though not completely, as I slip my hand beneath her chin, tilting her face to look upon mine.

"Come."

Wordlessly, she obeys as we both stand. Our hands intertwine as we weave through the large crowd. When we make it to the stairs, I hear the soft sound of Ryder giggling while Aries shouts. They're playing some kind of game. They're safe. They're okay. That's what matters.

It's not the end, though.

I walk into our temporary room, close the door behind us and lock it, then flick the bedroom light on.

"How many?" Blake asks.

She knows what will happen next; she's expected it because over time we've found it's what I need. I need to regain balance. I need my composure back. I need the darkness out of me, and I need it out now.

"As many as it takes," I say as I roll my sleeves up to my elbows.

Blake nods, moving to the end of the bed before peeling down her pants and panties and bending herself over the bed. I take a moment, admiring the sight of my beautiful wife. Her cunt is poking out in a way that has my cock twitching, her ass like a juicy peach ripe for the picking. This isn't sexual, though, not in this moment.

I step towards her, my hand rubbing against the smooth skin before I pull back, clapping down against her in a way that has her back bowing. She attempts to muffle her scream, but on the second and third spank, she's unable to do so. With each strike against her ass, the knot in my chest loosens. Her skin becomes hot beneath my touch, and I crave each strike like I crave my next breath.

Slowly, the anger inside me fades, the fear fueling it all

tempering until I'm left with my shaking wife in my lap, tears pouring down her face and her eyes filled with so much remorse. I needed this; she knows that, and I'll never be able to thank her for allowing Zayden and me to release our demons and loving us all the same.

I move my hand to her raw ass, skating it up her spine, then moving it to her face. I squeeze her cheeks together before forcing her to look back at me, then I slam my mouth to hers. My tongue darts out, catching a stray tear before I lick the hot trail it leaves behind. Blake whimpers before a soft moan slips from her lips.

When I pull away, our gazes lock, and I can't help but get lost in her beautiful eyes. One bright blue like Zayden's and one dark brown like my own. The perfect combination. The perfect woman.

Gently, I lift her into my arms, taking care not to touch where she's sore as I slowly walk us to the bathroom. With one arm, I reach down and start the flow of the deep bathtub, allowing the warm water to fill as I set her on her feet. Wordlessly, Blake lifts her arms so I can undress her fully before I begin undressing myself. As soon as we're both naked, I step into the tub, then pick her up once more before settling us into the warm water.

She straddles me as the water bites against her skin. She winces, sinking her mouth into my shoulder to muffle her moans. Once she becomes used to the feeling, I gently move her to settle above my cock before slowly pressing her down onto it. A gasp escapes her as I roll my head back, taking my time with this moment, with her.

Once she's fully seated on me, I grip her hips gently, carefully lifting her up and down on me as her arms wind around my neck.

"Dom," she whimpers.

"Yeah, babygirl?"

"I'm sorry," she cries. "I'm so sorry. I didn't think."

I nod, allowing her to feel all she feels before I speak.

"The thought of losing you... it's unfathomable. Unimaginable.

You often forget Zayden's heart isn't the only one that beats for you."

She looks to me, her eyes drenched with emotion as she shakes her head. "I never forget."

I lift a hand to the back of her neck and pull her to me as our lips touch. We stay like that for several moments, succumbing to our embrace, only the gentle motions of our lovemaking echoing in the quiet bathroom. Each thrust brings us closer and closer, and the instant her tongue swirls around mine is the very moment my cock throbs inside her.

Together, we fall over the cliff of pleasure, practically pulling it out of one another. We gasp and moan, grinding our bodies in a way that wrings out every drop of ecstasy possible.

When we pull away, her head rests against my water-dotted chest. No words are exchanged; neither of us have ever felt the need to fill silence with useless chatter. When we speak, it's intentional, meaningful.

"I love you," she mutters, still pressed against me.

My arms wind tighter around her as I press a soft kiss to the top of her head. "I love you more."

Chapter Sixteen
Ronan

After Dominic took Blake upstairs to—what sounded like—torture her, Zayden went to check on his kids, accompanied by Skyla and Liam while Asher sorted out dinner with Wesley. Me? I went straight to the computer and began pulling up everything I could on the man in the back of our car and the accomplices in the SUV.

Facial recognition has pulled up nothing so far, but I'm hoping the fancy biometric scanner that Asher acquired recently may point us in some kind of direction.

The door opens and closes, my best friend swaggering in like it's any other day before he tosses something at my chest.

I catch it easily, looking down at the object. "What's this?"

"Dead guy's finger," he says as he takes a seat and kicks his feet up on the desk.

"Wes, what the fuck?" I bark, tossing the severed finger onto the desk before looking for the scanner.

"What did you find on the car?" Wesley asks.

"Nothing," I grunt as I dig around the boxes at my feet.

I swear to fuck no one ever cleans up after themselves around here, and I'm fucking sick of it.

"Let me take a look into it," he says.

"I've looked. They're fake plates. It's a dead end."

Leaning forward and resting his elbows against the desk, he smirks. "Well, maybe I'm better than you."

I look over at him, shaking my head in irritation as I go back to my search for this fucking scanner. "You're cute," I snark.

I can practically hear his frown in his words as he speaks.

"Are you... mad at me?"

I huff out a breath but don't respond. Goddamnit. I swear I just saw it over—

"Got it," I say to myself as I plug the scanner in and hook it up to the computer.

I pull up the FBI database that Wesley "let himself into" a few months ago and sync the scanner to it as he speaks again.

"Ro."

I ignore him once more, grabbing the finger and pressing it to the scanner as it whirrs to life. Matches begin appearing on the computer screen, and I keep my eyes focused on it until a hand grips my jaw, forcing my gaze away from it.

"Ronan," Wesley says, a deep frown marring his otherwise happy-go-lucky features. "What's wrong?"

"Besides the fact that our wife could have been kidnapped today?" I say with a laugh that holds no humor.

"Yeah, besides that. You're upset with me. I just can't figure out why."

I try to look anywhere except at him, but his hold on me is too strong and unyielding. His pale blue eyes practically drill into me, and before I can stop myself, I'm speaking.

"You took off. You had no idea what kind of potential danger you were in; you had no regard for your safety. No backup. You were just... gone."

Wesley tilts his head to the side like he still doesn't see the problem. He doesn't fucking get it.

"Forget it," I huff, shaking my head and pushing him away.

He lets me go as I look to see the screen is still sorting through possible matches before he forces himself in front of me once more.

"Look at me," he says.

Still, I refuse him. I don't want to look at him. I don't know what I'll do, what I'll say. I prefer to keep things bottled up where they belong, especially when I don't know what to do with them. Especially when they're all like... this.

His hand moves to the back of my hair, tugging on the short strands the best he can as he snaps, "Look. At. Me."

My eyes move to his before I can stop myself, and once they do, I know it's all over.

"I was scared earlier. I still am. The fear hasn't left, and I'm... I'm dealing," I admit.

Wesley's grip on my hair loosens slightly but not all the way. He tilts his head slightly. "I know, but you kept Skyla safe. You kept them both safe. They're okay."

I let out an irritated laugh as I shake my head. "I wasn't scared for Sky; I was scared for you, you fucking moron. I was scared of what would happen to you! That I would lose you. That I would never be able to—"

My words die on my tongue as I force my jaw shut.

Wesley's eyes widen in surprise before they soften. "Ro, I..."

"Are you going to make me fucking say it?" I snap.

He stays quiet for a moment, his eyes flicking back and forth between each of mine before he shakes his head, lowering his tone.

"We've been best friends for two decades—you don't have to say anything."

I swallow roughly as he closes the distance between us. Wesley and I have kissed plenty of times, fucked even more. It's always been a sort of... release. A primal thing. There have never been...

feelings. At least I haven't wanted there to be any. But the instant his lips touch mine, everything changes. My stomach dips the way it does when I kiss Skyla. Euphoria washes over me when he crawls into my lap, just the way it does when I hold her. These feelings that I've been fighting for so goddamn long are banging at the door, and now I'm fucking terrified they won't be going anywhere anytime soon.

Wesley's grip on me tightens as he pulls us closer together, our tongues battling for dominance. He's kissing me like it could be our last time, like I'm ready to run. Fuck me, I don't want to run. Not from him. Not ever.

"Ro," he pants into my mouth, forcing my cock to jolt against him.

"I can't lose you," I admit as he moves his lips against my cheek, then peppers my neck with kisses, sucking on that sensitive part that has my toes curling.

"You never will," he promises against my skin.

"I could have. I need you, Wes. I..."

He freezes, pulling back slightly to look at me. I do my best to regain my composure, but I'm the first to admit I'm fucking terrible at it right now. Swallowing roughly, I bring one of my hands to his neck, holding him in place as I speak.

"Bend over for me. Now," I strain.

Wesley practically jumps out of my lap, and I'm standing behind him in an instant. He moves to undo his jeans, but I stop him, plastering my cock against his ass and gently grinding against him. Fuck. He feels so good against me.

I push his hands out of the way and undo his belt with one hand, freeing the button of his jeans before I reach inside and take what I want. His cock throbs in my hand as I grip him tightly, dragging my hand up and down the length several times before he rests his head against my shoulder and sighs.

"You like that?" I mutter into his ear.

His eyes lazily come to mine, so many words swirling within them. "I love it."

My heart practically leaps out of my chest as I release his cock, quickly undoing my own pants before pulling his all the way down. My hand comes to his back, and I bend him over the desk before spitting on his asshole.

"Hold on—this is gonna hurt," I warn as I push inside him.

He tenses beneath me, a murmured grunt barely escaping him as I fully seat myself inside him. I pull out slowly, spitting on my cock this time before pushing in easier. Normally we have lube at the ready. In every inch of all of our houses it feels like. Since kids, though, we've all had to be a little less adventurous in where we have sex. The only reason I feel safe in here with the door unlocked is because there are half a dozen adults out there keeping an eye on the kids. So that means right now, this moment, it's just us. Only us.

I push my cock in and out of Wesley as he reaches down and begins fisting his dick. He moans and bucks his ass against me, begging for more.

"You feel so good," he moans.

"So do you," I say through clenched teeth.

My hands are wrapped around his hips so that I can control the pace, but I quickly move one so that I can stroke his cock. Wes lets me, moving his hands to grip the desk as I begin quickly stroking him.

"You feel like mine," I admit before I can stop myself.

Wesley turns his head to look at me as I continue pounding away inside him. His eyes are filled with heat and want as he speaks.

"All yours, Ronan."

My cock twitches, and a rush of pleasure runs through me as I pick up my pace.

"Fuck! I love this. I love us. I love you, Wesley. I think I've loved you for so long. I've tried to fight it. Tried to bury it," I ramble as my orgasm begins to creep up on me.

I jerk Wesley faster, desperate to have him come with me.

His words are stuttered and shaky as he nods and moans.

"Me too. I love you. So much. So, so much. I want you, Ro, just like this, forever."

His words are my total undoing. My balls draw up before I release inside him, fucking him harder as I milk every bit of my orgasm that I can. Wesley lets out a louder shout before his cum covers the desk. His hips buck against me, forcing me to lengthen my strokes on him as he continues to moan and wiggle against me.

When we're both more than spent, we collapse. He slumps against the desk as I cover his back with my chest. We lie there for a countless amount of time, just breathing.

Eventually, we slowly peel ourselves away from one another before he turns to face me. The air is heavy, thick with tension as he watches me carefully. I swallow, expecting... I don't really know. I don't even know what just happened. One minute I was sitting here, and the next I was... confessing things I swore I never would. Feelings I insisted I never had. Skyla has reassured me countless times over the years that she would be more than comfortable with Wesley and I having more of a... romantic partnership, much like Asher and Liam. I always brushed her off, though. I always brushed everyone off. What started as a release while Skyla was with her other husbands turned into... more. I found myself craving Wesley. Craving his time, his laugh, his body. I've been craving him for years now, and in this moment, I'm struggling to remember why I've denied myself such pleasure. Why I've been denying us both.

He doesn't speak; doesn't ask questions or demand answers. Instead, Wesley takes two steps until our chests brush together before he cups my face in his hands.

"There's no running out on me now, Ronan. I love you, and now you're stuck with me forever."

How do I tell him that running out on him has never crossed my mind? That it never will? How do I tell him that now that I've been cracked open, raw and bare like this, that nothing will ever stop me from having him, just like nothing could ever stop me from having Skyla. I now have a fuller clarity on how she can love so many of us equally. I love him just as much as I do her, like two halves of my heart are finally clicking into place.

"Forever," I agree.

Chapter Seventeen
Asher

Ronan and Wesley were able to pull a fingerprint match on the prick that was following Skyla and Blake. Alexander Coombs. Born and raised in Philly, in and out of juvenile detention nine times by the time he turned eighteen, followed by three stints in prison, all in his short thirty-two years of life.

Most of his crimes were stupid shit. Petty theft, breaking and entering. Though according to records, he died in a mysterious house fire three years ago. Clearly, that was fucking bullshit because he was alive and well just this morning. Until his own guys shot him in the fucking head.

I gotta be honest, we're all a little to blame. We let Sky twist our arms. I don't think any of us were overly comfortable with the idea of them leaving the house, but she stuck out her lower lip and batted her eyes, and just like that, I was a weak fucker ready to give her anything and everything that she wanted. Liam and I hung at home with the kids watching Christmas movies and burning Christmas cookies—twice, thanks to Liam the chef. All the while not having a clue that our wife was in danger.

It doesn't help that on top of all this shit going on with the

Graves family, Hutchinson has been fucking up. I get that his wife just had a baby, but that doesn't give him an excuse to ignore his job. He's head of cybersecurity, and twice this week alone, we've had data leaks. Not that I've admitted that to anyone besides the two of us. That information would only cause panic, and some things not all the Elders need to be privy to.

"Hey!" Liam says, bouncing towards me before jumping onto the couch.

I look up from my phone, raising an eyebrow in question as he grins. "Yes?"

"I swindled Ronan and Wesley into bedtime duty, which means with the way Jackson has been stalling lately, we should have a solid forty-five minutes of fun time!" he says with a smirk.

"Fun time?" I ask. He's holding much more of my attention now than he did just a moment ago.

"Mhmm. I've got a surprise since we were all naughty," he teases. "Meet you upstairs in five!" And he practically skips off to the garage.

I shake my head, only for a moment wondering why I love that goofy fucker. The smile on my face quickly reminds me, though.

As I climb the stairs, I see Blake, Zayden and Dominic all discussing something quietly, Blake's arms crossed over her chest as Dominic massages her shoulders and Zayden nods seriously. If I wasn't so goddamn exhausted with everything going on, I might be nosey enough to snoop on them. As it turns out, a little relaxation—or fun time—with my wife and boyfriend sounds a lot more appealing.

When I push inside our bedroom, I find Skyla already lying on the bed, a little black camisole dress practically wrapped around her body. She's so fucking gorgeous. I still don't know how I got so lucky. How any of us got so lucky.

The shower is on in the bathroom, the door slightly ajar.

"Griggs?" I ask.

She nods with a soft smile.

"Tough shit for him—you're mine and Liam's tonight," I say as I slide onto the bed, pulling her to lie on top of me, careful not to squish the baby.

She giggles as she pushes her hair out of her face, smiling down at me lovingly. "I think he might have something to say about that."

"Let him," I reply with a shrug before cupping the back of her head and pulling her lips down to mine.

She smiles against me, and when we pull apart, she nuzzles her head into my neck. We lie there for a moment, my hand absent-mindedly rubbing her back before she speaks.

"I'm sorry for today."

"It's fine, princess. I think we all underestimated just how closely they're being watched. None of us anticipated them already tracking the Graves family up here."

"Still..." She shrugs. "I feel bad. Blake is kinda lonely. I can tell. I was just trying to cheer her up."

I laugh. "She has two husbands who're obsessed with her—how lonely can she get?"

Skyla pulls away to look at me with a steady gaze. "Love and friendship are two different cups, and they don't always fill each other up."

I nod at that. She has a point, and with the way Zayden and Dominic treat her, I doubt she's ever let out of their sight, let alone allowed to have friends. Skyla doesn't have many friends either, though. She has Maggie of course, and by extension Bridgette sometimes, which is still a fucking trip for me, let me tell you. She does like Abigail, Andrew Hutchinson's wife, though I wouldn't necessarily call them friends. They mingle at Brethren gatherings, and Hutchinson tries to act like he still doesn't have a crush on my wife. Annoying little fuck.

I rest my hands on her belly and rub my thumbs against her gently. I know this baby is mine—there's no way it could be anyone else's. Not scientifically at least. Okay, maybe scientifically, but probability-wise, it's mine. Don't get me wrong, I love all my children equally; I always will, but something in me thrums with the excitement at the idea of fathering one of our children. That our whole family will be made up of small pieces of us blended together.

"I'm glad you both are safe."

Skyla smiles at me. "I swear, my ankles are already blowing up and it's winter. It's kinda bullshit."

I smile at her irritation before rolling her off me and scooting myself down to cup her feet. Slowly, I begin massaging her ankles, moving into her feet in a way that has her moaning in delight.

"Fuck, can this be your job for the rest of this pregnancy?"

I laugh at that. "Just this, princess?"

"Yeah, the others can handle everything else. You're on foot-rub duty."

I smile at that, more than happy to do whatever she needs to get her through this difficult time. The amount of joy she brings me each day just by existing is priceless. The fact that she's bringing another child of ours into the world? Repayment could never be achieved.

Unfortunately, all the joy is sucked from me when my phone rings. As much as I don't want to, I pause rubbing Skyla's feet and answer it.

"Yeah?"

"Sorry to bother you so late. I just... I found something, and I'm looking into it. I just don't know the origin of the entry point, and—"

"Cut to the fucking chase," I snap at Hutchinson.

"We've been hacked. Again."

"What?" I snarl.

"I know. I'm working on more firewalls. Extra precautions, but they... they only tapped into certain things," he stammers.

"Like?"

The line is quiet for a moment before he speaks.

"The security cameras to your private residence in Salem... and in New Hampshire."

Motherfucker.

"Cut their access now or I'll cut off your fucking head!" I shout. "I swear to God if you don't fix this shit, and quick, I'll be sending Griggs after you. This is your final fucking warning."

I end the call abruptly and toss the phone to the other side of the room. I swear, just because I'm not as big a prick as my father, people think they can slack off. That they can get away with shit. I am the leader of one of the most powerful secret societies in the world—that doesn't get handed to you by pussyfooting around and giving every jackass moron chance after chance. Lineage or not. If he doesn't fix our security leak, and soon, I will personally end the entire Hutchinson lineage with a goddamn smile on my face.

"Is everything okay?" Skyla asks with a frown.

I turn to face her, shaking my head. "No."

"Do you need to go?"

Yes.

"No, princess. I'm not going anywhere. You said it yourself. I'm on foot rub-duty."

Chapter Eighteen
Zayden

After Dominic did an extensive deep dive, we found out everything we needed to know about Alexander Coombs. Including the home address of his brother, who resides just outside New York City. I cut off his head and a few other body parts before I shoved them into a sack, then we made the road trip to his brother's house. You never know when he might be in the mood for a family reunion! Especially if he doesn't feel like chatting with us. I can't lie, walking around with a sack of body parts during Christmastime makes me feel a little like Santa. Maybe I'll even assemble them neatly beneath the Christmas tree if we have the time for it.

Before we left, I also packed a goodie bag. I've been trying to tame the demons inside me when we're at the house for my kids' sake, but that piece of shit threatened my family. He sent pictures of my wife to the very man after her, after us all, so naturally every person he's ever come into contact with should die a slow death. That being said, there's no reason I shouldn't get to have a little fun with it—it's the holidays after all!

Griggs drives us to the brother's shitty-ass apartment. It's in a sketchy part of town, so you'd really think he'd have better locks on his door. Alas, it takes no effort at all to pick the lock, and soon I'm tiptoeing into the house with two sacks over my shoulder. I have an eager smirk on my face to complete the moment, really making me feel like a dupe of the Grinch or something.

Because I can't help myself, I start humming under my breath before a hand smacks the back of my head.

"Are you seriously humming *The Grinch* theme song?" Dominic hisses.

"I'm getting into the holiday spirit!" I whisper with a smile.

He shoots me an outraged look, then glances around us. "We're on a fucking job—get your head in the game."

I look him up and down with disgust. "Your attitude," I say with a shake of my head. "Hate, hate, hate... LOATHE entirely."

"Zayden," he grits out.

I laugh lightly, shaking my head as I continue walking. Why does he always have such a stick up his ass? According to Dominic's research, Phillip Coombs lives alone with no partner or kids, so it really is simple.

Dom went over the plan about a hundred fucking times in the car—we have to question him first—as if he knows how bloodthirsty I am. Like he knows that the demons inside of me are clawing at my flesh, begging to be released.

Griggs and Dominic scan the place, weapons drawn, while I skip through the house. There's no need for all of that. I have not a doubt in the world this sad sack is unsuspecting as hell. To prove myself right, I push open the bedroom door and find a prematurely balding man with a keg for a belly stretching a white sweat-stained tank top. The room has an odor that doesn't please me, and I wrinkle my nose at the offensive smell. What is wrong with some men? A bar of soap is *not* the enemy.

I turn to Griggs and Dominic as I shake my head. "Grab Stinky and bring him into the living room. I'm not working in there," I say as I move to the living room, where I set my bags beside the Christmas tree, then take my time unpacking my goodies.

I hear a gasp of surprise come from the room before the sound of struggling. Then Griggs is dragging him across the floor by what little hair he has left and Dominic sets him in a chair. Moving around the Christmas tree, I find the plug and push it into the outlet. The entire room illuminates with colored lights, and I clap my hands, prepared to get to work.

"Rope," Griggs says.

I nod as I reach into my bag and hand him the rope I grabbed, though I did dress it up a bit.

"Red garland?" Dominic asks, assessing the sparkly rope.

"Garland wrapped around rope," I reply as I begin tying him to the chair with it.

Griggs and Dominic both exchange a look and shake their heads before Phillip begins babbling.

"What's going on? Where am I? What do you want?"

"That's entirely dependent on what you can give us, Phillip Morris Coombs, born at St. Martha's Hospital in Philadelphia, Pennsylvania, on September 9th at 6:42 PM—6lbs 2oz."

"So he wasn't always a fat fuck?" I ask.

"Not at all," Dominic says before looking back to the man who's as white as a ghost.

"H-how do you know me? Why are you here?" he stumbles.

"We're here for... information," Dominic says cryptically. "Your survival is dependent upon the helpfulness of your information, so let's just cut to it, shall we?"

He nods shakily as Dominic tilts his head to the side with curiosity.

"Your brother recently was given orders to follow a woman. Why?"

Phillip frowns, shaking his head. "I don't know. I don't talk to my brother."

Dominic just looks at me, as if giving me permission, and I practically skip over to him, delivering a hearty punch to his mouth that has a few teeth skittering across the floor before Dom continues.

"Let's try that again because either your phone company is lying, or you are. I saw records of you having a phone call with him just yesterday morning."

His eyes frantically move between the three of us before his muscles flex like he's attempting to free himself. When he realizes he can't strong-arm his way out of this, he heaves a few breaths and shakes his head. "I don't know. I don't know much. I—"

I match my last hit on his other side, keeping him even of course. Blood runs out of his mouth and down his chin as Griggs grabs him by the throat, snarling into his face.

"Cut the shit or we'll end your pathetic life right here and now."

I pout at that. I'll be seriously pissed if they take away my fun with a bullet to the head. I'm already annoyed that I didn't get to let out some much-needed frustration on his dear old brother. This tight-lipped fucker isn't saying shit, though.

Shaking my head, I crouch down to my other bag as I speak over my shoulder. "He's not going to talk, guys. He's loyal. You'll talk to your brother, though, right?"

"Alex? He's here?" Phillip pants. "Y-yeah. Yeah, I'll talk. If Alex says it's okay, I'll talk."

I nod at that. Perfect.

As fast as I'm able, I stick my hand inside Alexander's head, fashioning it to fit into his jaw like it's a puppet. I may or may not have hollowed out part of his head at the house with the very intention of doing this. It actually looks creepy as fuck, the stuff nightmares are made of. I can't help but giggle at how completely fucked up it is, but I've always wanted to try my hand at ventriloquism.

Ha. Get it? Try my hand?

When I turn around, I push the head puppet out in front of Phillip's face and do my best not to move my mouth as I work Alexander's jaw.

"Please, Phillip! Tell them what they want to know. It's okay, I won't be mad."

Horror claws itself across Phillip's face, his brain clearly struggling to put together what his eyes are seeing.

"Zayden, what the fuck?" Dominic sighs.

"That's fucking disgusting," Griggs says with a grimace.

I can't help but snicker as I focus on our target, who looks like he's about to blow chunks all over himself. I worked really hard on that garland. If he pukes on it, I'm gonna be pissed.

"Y-you killed him," Phillip strangles out, a tear falling down his face.

"Actually no!" I say as I look at the head, working the jaw some more as I do. "I know it looks bad and all, but do you see this hole right here?" I say as I move the head puppet closer, just inches away from his face.

Phillip attempts to lean away from it, trying to look anywhere but at him... or it... or whatever.

"That wasn't from us. That was from his buddies. Yeah, turns out he wasn't a track star when it came to evading, and when they thought he was going to get caught, they shot him and drove away. Any idea who those guys might have been?"

He looks to me with surprise. "Jacob killed him?"

Dom takes a step back, his fingers now flying across his phone screen.

"It would appear so. Does Jacob have a last name?" I ask.

Phillip shakes his head. "I don't know it. Alex started working with him when..."

"When Desmond Volkov faked his death and employed him?" Griggs fills in.

He looks to Griggs with surprise, like he's confused how we

could possibly get that kind of information. I see why Desmond only picked up the one brother—this one is dumber than a box of rocks.

"You got an address for Jacob? A phone number?" I ask.

He shakes his head, and my patience begins to slip. I toss the puppet to the side—because even with my gloves, it's starting to make my fingers pruney, and I absolutely hate that feeling—then grip his face with my blood-soaked glove.

The head hits the ground with a thunk before doing a quarter roll. Ironically, the eyes stay open and are pointed directly at Phillip. Phillip's eyes stay on Alexander's before moving to mine.

"He said Desmond wanted him to follow a girl. That intel said she'd be vulnerable. He was supposed to confirm the target and then grab her. Kill anyone who got in his way."

For a moment, my joy slips as I allow his words to sink in properly. "And do what with her?" I ask as my body begins to shake.

He shakes his head. "Wait for further instruction."

An eye for an eye. That's what Desmond was thinking no doubt. I killed his sister, so he wants to kill my wife, probably torture her. Maybe worse.

I release Phillip's face with a rough shake, then take a step back, turning to my goodie bag.

"That's all I know, I swear," Phillip says as I turn back around, this time with a meat cleaver in my hand.

"I know." If his brother had been working for the Four Horsemen for this long, he wasn't a snitch, meaning he wouldn't have told his brother much to begin with. I'm honestly surprised he told him even that much.

"Please!" he begs as I take a step closer. "I've told you everything I know!"

"I'm sure you have. Thank you for that. Oh, and happy holidays," I say before I pull my hand back and swing true.

The cleaver is surprisingly sharp and almost cuts through the neck with one swipe. It's still kinda holding on by some muscle and skin, but a few more hacks and his head also hits the ground with a thud before rolling towards his brother's.

"Aw, that's kinda cute. Even in death, they've got each other's back. You think that will be us, Dom?"

He scoffs, continuing to type on his phone. "You planning to get decapitated by a psycho with a cleaver while you're bound to a chair by Christmas decorations?"

I shrug. "There are certainly less interesting ways to die."

"Can we focus here?" Griggs asks with a huff. "We really don't have anything new to go off. We have the first name of one of the accomplices. So what?"

"So nothing," Dominic says.

Griggs frowns as Dominic pockets his phone. "What? We drove our asses out here to kill a man for nothing but secondary revenge?"

Dominic nods. "That and Zayden needed to have a little fun."

I nod in agreement, smiling at Griggs as he looks at me like I'm deranged. Rude but fair.

"So what's the plan now? Are we just sitting around with our thumbs in our asses or...?" Griggs snarks.

"Goddamn, Griggs. You need to lighten up, get in the spirit of things. I swear to God, you act like you don't even enjoy the kill."

"I don't," he says flatly. "It's a job. A means to an end."

I smirk at that, shaking my head as I tsk. "You can lie to a lot of people, but not to us. I see through your bullshit surly façade. You're as warped as I am."

"Well," Dominic hedges.

I look over my shoulder at him. "Fair enough. Almost. You crave the kill whether you like to admit it or not. Once you take as many lives as we have, it changes a person. You couldn't just wake up and not do it anymore, trust me—you'd earn yourself a one-way ticket to the looney bin. You need it just like I do."

Griggs frowns at my words, like he doesn't want to admit the truth in them. Why? I wonder. Does he think he can't have a happy life and be a mercenary? I'm living proof that you can. I have a beautiful wife, the best brother anyone could ask for and two beautiful twins. My life is perfect. Maybe he just needs to stop fighting the darkness and succumb. I bet he'd smile a hell of a lot more.

Chapter Nineteen
Liam

"Tape," I ask as I hold out my hand.

"Tape." Seraphina smiles as she hands it to me.

I nod, taping the seam of the reindeer-print wrapping paper.

"Bow," I ask.

Jackson hands me a bow, a wide smile on his face. "Bow."

"Label," I ask next, and Brooks looks to me, more to-and-from labels on his body than left on the sheet.

Seraphina rolls her eyes and peels one off his forehead before handing it to me. After a quick scribble of Skyla's name, I hand the present to Ryder. Or Aries. Fuck, I can't tell them apart honestly.

"Will you go put that under the tree, big man?"

He nods like it's the most important task he's ever been given before running out into the living room while the other one—Aries or Ryder, I don't fucking know—is wrestling with wrapping a present he made for his parents. The other day while I was watching the kids, they were talking about Christmas and unsure what they could do for their parents. We looked up some easy homemade crafts and, with Seraphina's artistic flair, made some pretty cute things. Homemade picture frames out of popsicle sticks with a picture I took of the boys and printed, and a few knives that have had their handles bedazzled.

Now before you come for me, of course I didn't buy six-year-olds knives. They found them, and Seraphina did the bedazzling. You could tell the boys weren't sure about it at first, but at her insistence, they conceded.

I won't lie, if I didn't know who their parents were, I'd be judging a bit. Knowing their dads, it kinda tracks. Don't know if it's healthy per se for your children to know weapons are your favorite things, but who am I to judge?

"Daddy, Aries needs help," Seraphina says.

Got it. Aries green shirt, Ryder blue shirt. For today at least. Could we get them to stay in these clothes for the rest of their time with us? Or maybe we could get some really small tattoos to tell them apart? That's what I'd do if we had twins!

Okay, maybe not, but there is some validity to that idea.

I slide over towards the kids, take the cardboard box from him and quickly adjust the wrapping because duh, I'm not gonna let them just wrap a knife. It'll tear through the paper!

The second the paper is secured, the door to the playroom opens and we all freeze before each person quickly dives on top of an unwrapped present.

"GET OUTTTTT!" we shout as one.

Blake startles, throwing her hands in the air as the boys add, "Presents! Look away, Mama!"

Her hands fly to cover her eyes in an instant. "Sorry! Sorry! I just wanted to check on you guys."

I do a quick inventory of what we have left to wrap and determine that all the presents for her and her husbands are done.

"Stand down, troops—Operation Present Wrapping is still secure," I say to them. "Looks like we only have two presents left to wrap for Skyla and one for Asher."

The kids all sit up, literally relaxing like soldiers at ease. Have I mentioned how much I love being a dad? How much I love my kids? Because I love it so fucking much.

Now she's allowed to look, Blake slowly moves her hands from her face and smiles. "Have you guys been having fun?" she asks her kids.

"Yeah! We made presents," Green Shirt, I mean Aries, says, and Ryder finishes. "And then we wrapped them."

"And I helped!" Seraphina says, grinning up at Blake.

Blake smiles down at our little girl sweetly, then presses a kiss to the tops of her boys' heads before sitting down.

"Sounds like you've been keeping them entertained despite all the... heavy," she says carefully.

I shrug simply as I get back to work, wrapping the bottle of Scotch I got Asher. It's a rare one he's been trying to collect for years. No idea why—liquor is only good if you're allowed to drink it in my opinion, but it's not my Christmas present.

"Thank you," she whispers softly. "I appreciate it... We all do."

I smile at her. "It's not a problem; I'm typically the comedic relief of the group. Happy to fulfill my role."

She laughs at that and nods. "I don't doubt that for a second."

"How are you doing with... everything?" I say cryptically as my eyes drift down to her stomach.

Her eyes widen as she looks around to make sure the kids aren't listening. "Skyla told you?"

I shake my head. "She'd never, but I'm good at this thing. I'm four for four on calling her pregnancies before she even knew. It's like a fifth sense or something."

She nods before furrowing her brow. "Sixth sense, you mean."

"No, not the movie," I reply with a shake of my head before I think on my words. "Wait."

Blake busts up laughing, a true belly laugh that shakes her from her head to her toes. The kids join in on the laughter, and fuck it, so do I. I may be a dumbass sometimes, but at least I bring people joy, right?

We're laughing so hard that we don't hear the door open.

"What's so funny?" Skyla demands, her head poked around the door.

Yet again, we all scream—Blake included this time—and quickly attempt to cover Skyla's remaining presents.

"GET OUTTTT!"

"Agh! Sorry!" she says as she scrambles out of the room, calling through the doorway. "Jackson requested we do a cocoa bar, and I was just coming to let you guys know it's all set up."

"COCOAAA!" Jackson cheers as he jumps to his feet, pulling his little brother up with him. They take off running through the door.

I laugh as I watch them go, Seraphina and the twins quickly following behind.

"I'm almost done in here!" I call out as Blake stands and heads out with everyone.

Once the last present is wrapped, I clean up the supplies and grab all the presents, setting them underneath the Christmas tree. Well, I try. These kids are so fucking spoiled, and having six adults that live together already creates an abundance of gifts during the holidays. Factor in four kids and our new guests, and, well, all I can say is thank God I fuck one of the richest men in the country because my trust fund couldn't hang with this shit.

Speak of the devil.

Someone smacks my ass, and I turn to see Asher standing behind me. I stand up straight to face him, smirking as I look up at him.

"You know the rules: you smack it, you fuck it," I tease with a waggle of my brows.

"Don't tempt me," he grumbles before placing a kiss to my lips.

Fuck, I love him.

When he pulls away, he shoots me a wink that sends my heart beating out of rhythm before he moves over to Skyla at the cocoa bar. Wrapping an arm around her, he presses a kiss to her neck before she moves to put on a Christmas movie.

Once the kids are settled, us grown-ups all get our own hot chocolates. Asher and I pour a healthy amount of booze into ours.

"Blake?" Asher offers.

I scoff. "You trying to give away all my booze? I'm on an allowance!"

Asher gives me a "you're an idiot" look before lifting the bottle in offering once more. She just smiles and shakes her head no, so Asher puts it back in the liquor cabinet.

Chapter Twenty
Blake

I like Liam. If I had to choose a favorite of Skyla's men, it would absolutely be Liam. Maybe it's because he kind of reminds me of Zayden—the humor part, hold the unhinged. Or maybe it's because he's been a godsend with the kids. Every time I turn around, he's playing some game or baking something with them. Doing anything to distract them from the fact that their dads have basically been MIA since we arrived at this house full of strangers just before Christmas.

I know it's nearly impossible for me to keep them completely sheltered from this life. I mean, this is our life. It's one that we've all chosen, and there's no changing it. I think it's the least I can do as a mother to try, though.

We all sit back, casually chatting as we watch the kids watch the movie. Well, Jackson and Brooks are watching the movie. My boys are currently fussing over Seraphina, getting her pillows, blankets and doing everything they can to make her comfortable, and that little girl is eating it up. I don't know if they're behaving this way because they see their dads acting like that with me or what, but it's fucking adorable.

We only make it twenty minutes into the movie before a fight breaks out, which, honestly, is a record for them.

"Move!" Aries snaps.

"I did," Ryder scoffs.

"You're still touching her!" Aries says before he shoves Ryder away from Seraphina.

Ryder looks away, clearly trying to conceal his tears as Seraphina looks to Aries.

"You need to say sorry! You hurt his feelings."

Aries looks at her and shakes his head. "I'm not gonna say sorry. He's being a baby."

"I am not!" Ryder says, then jumps over Seraphina and pushes Aries. It quickly turns into a scrap, and Asher, myself and Liam all move forward. Liam extracts Seraphina from the middle; Asher holds Aries back as I grip Ryder.

"That's enough. Cool it," Asher says in a tone that brokers no discussion.

Both of the boys fall quiet as they look at him before Ryder tears out of my grip and runs for the stairs.

I let out a heavy sigh as I turn to Aries. "You will be apologizing to your brother in the morning. Go brush your teeth and head to bed."

"The movie isn't over!" he argues.

I widen my eyes at him as the movie instantly turns off.

"Bedtime, kids. Let's hit it," Skyla says.

Several groans of protest sound from the couch, but I look to her and mouth, "Thank you," before heading upstairs to track down Ryder.

When I step into the boys' room, I don't see him at first, but I hear him. Soft sniffling sounds come through the window, and I look to see it cracked open and Ryder sitting out on the flat roof.

"Ryder, get inside right now! You're gonna fall!" I snap.

He looks at me and frowns before slowly coming back through

the window. He always does this at our house in Seattle, and that doesn't have a flat roof. Don't come for me—we've literally had to bar his windows. He likes being outside, looking at the stars, and he's going to give me a fucking heart attack one of these days.

As soon as he's inside, I lock the window behind him before shutting the curtains. He's standing in front of me with his arms crossed over his chest and a pout twisting at his features.

"Do you want to talk about it?" I ask as I crouch down in front of him.

"Aries is a jerk," he mutters.

I can't help but laugh at that, shaking my head. "He's not a jerk, sweetheart."

His deep brown eyes come to me in frustration. "He's always picking on me. I wasn't even touching her."

I let out a soft sigh as I rub his back. "You know your daddies always fought like this as kids too. It's what brothers do unfortunately. It's okay to speak up and tell him that you don't like the way he's treating you; it's not okay to retaliate."

"What's that mean?"

I smile and huff. "Hit him back."

"But that's not fair!" he argues.

"Life isn't fair, babe. Aries will be punished for pushing you, but now you're in trouble too."

He mutters under his breath, but I'm unable to make any of his words out.

"You both need to try to be a little kinder to each other. You're family."

"I wish Seraphina was my family instead."

I don't know how to respond to that, but luckily I don't have to as he continues.

"Do we have to leave? Can't we stay with them?"

I smile sadly. "You like it here, Ry?"

He nods as I do the same.

"Me too. We're not leaving just yet, so enjoy the time you have, okay?"

"Okay."

"Alright, go brush your teeth."

He does so, begrudgingly, and I look to see Dominic is in the doorway watching me with a soft smile.

"Hi."

I smile back. "Hi," I say as I stand. Then I walk towards him and he wraps his arms around me.

"Did you hear all that?" I mutter into his chest.

"That our sons are six and already fighting over a girl? Yeah, saw that coming."

I laugh at that. "Tell me it gets easier."

He slips his hand beneath my chin, forcing me to look at him as he speaks. "Afraid not."

Another laugh escapes me. True facts—I've got first-hand experience on that matter.

"I'm not sure there's any tearing these kids apart. When we're able to go home, that is," I say.

Dominic shrugs. "They'll get over it. Seattle to Salem isn't exactly a weekend drive."

That saddens me more than it should, which is stupid, I know. My stomach begins to twist and ache at the thought of leaving, which is so weird because I should be craving home more than anything. Home means we're safe, home means we're free. Instead...

I push out of Dominic's arms and tear towards the bathroom.

"Mommy?" Ryder asks as I barely make it to the toilet before emptying my entire stomach inside.

"Give us a second, Ry," Dominic says as he rubs my back soothingly.

My stomach heaves several more times before the nausea settles. Dom is watching me with concern and pursed lips. If I just threw up over the thought of leaving our newfound friends, that would be dramatic. Morning sickness didn't hit me this early with the twins. Glancing to Dom, I can practically read his every thought. I see the questions dancing through his head; I can feel the words on the tip of his tongue.

I shake my head, though, begging him not to ask, and to my relief, he doesn't. We just stay there and he continues rubbing my back until the sickness slowly eases.

I'll tell them. Soon. Just... not yet. Not when there are still three out of the Four Horsemen out for our heads. They don't need the extra pressure, the extra worries, and neither do I. Once I tell them... it's real, and though I'm coming round to the idea of it... I'm still terrified.

Chapter Twenty One
Wesley

I look down at my phone as a notification appears on the screen, followed by a security alert. I watch as the four cars fan out along our property line, tucking themselves in the street so they remain hidden. I can see them, though, and they're twenty-five minutes late, something I'll be taking up with my buddy. He owns one of the most elite private security companies in the country, and with the Four Horsemen not only after the Graves family but holding on to interior security footage of my family, I thought a little protection wouldn't hurt.

Asher didn't tell anyone about the leaked footage—per usual, he's trying to handle everything on his own. Sometimes he pulls it off, other times not so much. Ronan and I have come to the agreement that if he's going to run the Brethren for generations to come, he needs to learn to delegate. We can't force him to do so, but that doesn't mean I'm going to sit around and do nothing with this information. I didn't ask for permission because I didn't want to be met with resistance.

They need extra security because Zayden, Dominic and

Vincent are going after another one of the Horsemen, Andre Ivanov. We were able to capture a private jet itinerary that shows him landing in Paris in exactly six hours. It's an eleven-hour trip for us, which means we're already behind, but more ahead than we were with the last target.

I say *we* because last night, Dominic informed me that I would be joining them in London. He said he needed another babysitter to look after Zayden and Vincent so they don't paint the streets with blood, but I knew he was full of shit. He wants me by his side because he knows I have access to certain government databases he could only dream of breaking into. It pays to fight for your country and have active contacts to this day that are more loyal to you than their superiors.

Our only luggage is a backpack each. Asher has called in a private jet to meet us at the local airfield, and Zayden, Blake and Dominic are saying their goodbyes while Vincent does the same with Skyla. Ronan walks up to me, taking my bag from my hands before setting it into the back for me.

"Thanks," I say.

He nods. "Still don't know why they asked you to come and not me."

"It's because I'm better than you," I tease as I shut the trunk.

Ronan lifts an unimpressed eyebrow. "In what way?"

I smirk. "Every way."

He tries to hold on to his pinched, less-than-enthusiastic expression, but he can't do it, and a smile slowly slips across his face that sends my heart racing. He leans forward, resting a hand on my hip before pulling me closer. Surprise ripples through me. Typically, he's careful about when and where he shows me affection. It's rarely in front of others and usually only when we're naked. When his lips touch mine, though, it's anything but sexual. It's passionate, warm... perfect.

When he pulls away, he rests his forehead to mine. "Come home safe, yeah?"

I smile at that and nod. "Of course."

"I'll miss you," Skyla says from behind us.

We pull apart, both smiling down at her as she looks between us. A mischievous smile plays at her lips, like she somehow orchestrated this whole... thing between Ronan and me. Or at least she likes to think so and will be claiming credit. I don't care who takes credit for what; I'm just so deliriously happy, and I want it to stay that way.

"I'll miss you, little one. We'll be in and out. I'll see you by lunch tomorrow."

She nods, wrapping her arms around my neck. I try to pull her closer to me, but her growing belly is beginning to make that a little difficult. Ronan pushes me away from her slightly until I'm no longer pressed against her belly.

Rolling my eyes, I look to him and laugh. "Easy, papa bear. I'm not hurting your baby or woman."

"Our woman and baby, and yes you fucking were."

Skyla sighs at our bickering, lifting onto her tiptoes to place a kiss on my lips before taking Ronan's hand.

"Come on—you've been assigned back-rubbing duty," she says.

He follows after dutifully, both of them casting me last-minute smiles. I smile back, lifting my hand to wave when Dominic pauses beside me, clapping his hand on my shoulder.

"Let's go."

When we land in London, a car is already waiting for us. To the driver's credit, he didn't look in the back once. Not when Dominic was assembling the guns he took apart for the flight. Not when Zayden was actively sharpening knife after knife. Not even when

Vincent started pulling out every weapon fathomable from his bag, handing me a couple before strapping the rest to his body.

We're suiting up like we're going to battle. Granted, I've never been on a hit before, but I've been on plenty of missions, and this sure as shit feels like a mission. I guess technically it is.

"Do we have his itinerary?" I ask the car.

"No," Dominic says, loading a bullet into the chamber before beginning on the next gun. "Make yourself useful," he says, handing me half a dozen empty clips and a large box of bullets.

I begin loading each as Vincent speaks.

"We have a hotel reservation; that's all we need."

Dominic moves Zayden's bag, and it jingles. We all look to him with confusion as he grins. A mischievous childlike grin, something that Jackson or Brooks would wear when sneaking into something they ought not to.

"What the fuck is jingling, Zay?" Dominic asks, his tone oozing exhaustion with his twin.

"A little of this, a little of that."

When no one says anything, he tosses his hands out by his sides and snickers. "It's Christmastime! I'm being festive."

"Jesus," Vincent mutters under his breath and shakes his head.

I don't know him well enough to give him shit for anything. Besides, he seems a little too mentally unstable to be making any type of comments. He seems the type to laugh and joke one moment and slit your throat in the next breath. No, thanks. I'll just stay quiet and load clips.

Dominic screws on silencers to the guns before handing one to each of us.

We arrive at a nice hotel then and all exit the car, Vincent tossing the driver a wad of bills so fat, he won't even think of mentioning us to anyone. Or at least that's the idea.

We walk into the lobby and are immediately greeted by staff.

Dominic takes charge, throwing down a card onto the desk as he speaks.

"Grand suite, eastern-facing terrace."

The employee nods and smiles, then frowns. "I'm sorry, sir, we don't have any grand suites available on the eastern side. If you would like—"

"Check again," he says stiffly.

"But, sir—"

"Check again," he repeats.

She shakes her head but does as he says, surprise flashing across her face a moment later.

"My apologies."

Once she hands us our keys, we move to the elevator, riding it all the way to the top floor. We enter the room before heading straight for the terrace. Vincent grabs the patio table as Zayden moves the chairs, clearing a pathway before he takes a few steps back, then vaults up and over the ledge, landing on the other terrace. My eyes widen with surprise. It's not a far jump by any means, but we're thirty stories high and the gap is at least six feet. Vincent follows after easily before Dominic looks to me.

"You good?"

I nod, then he turns to his brother, getting a running start before jumping to the other terrace. Fuck, guess that just leaves me.

I back up as far as I'm able, leaping over the ledge and flying through the air. The only problem is my foot catches the edge, dragging me down. I reach out frantically and just barely grip a piece of the ledge on the other terrace.

Vincent's hand comes down in offering, and I take it before Dominic reaches over to grab my other. Together, they pull me up.

Zayden is sitting on the table, swinging his feet like he's bored. "I thought you said he was a SEAL, Griggs."

"I am," I say as my feet touch the terrace.

He shrugs. "Could have fooled me."

I scoff. "Well, my training didn't exactly consist of jumping from hotel terrace to terrace. Put me in the water and then say something."

My adrenaline is still thrumming from my almost death, and maybe I'm a little irritated by his superior attitude.

To my surprise, he doesn't get upset by my attitude. Instead, he looks at me consideringly before he shrugs. "Noted."

I frown at his casual indifference.

But he just jumps to his feet and opens the French doors easily, and we enter what I assume is Andre's hotel room. As a unit, Vincent, Zayden and Dominic begin setting up in different areas of the suite. Dominic is fastening something to the doorframe, Zayden and Vincent are laying out their plethora of weapons neatly, and I'm left standing there more than a little useless.

"What do you need me to do?" I ask.

"Watch the door. If someone comes through it, shoot them," Dominic says.

Can do.

A minute later, Zayden is hidden behind the bar, Dominic is tucked into the bar and Vincent is crouched behind the sofa in front of me. His hand reaches for my sleeve before he yanks hard, pulling me towards him.

"Can you let me in on what the fuck we're doing?" I scoff.

"Andre travels with a minimum of five security staff. Dominic placed a device on the door that we can lock once all are inside the room. Then it's just about killing them before they can kill us."

I look at him with surprise. "Seriously? That's your best plan?"

"You have a better one?" Vincent asks.

I shake my head and throw up my hands. "We're all putting ourselves in danger for no reason. We could have blown the place up, or tear-gassed them at the very least, or... I don't know. Dead is dead, right? We don't have to feel the life drain with our hands, do we?"

"That's half the fun!" Zayden calls out from the other side of the room.

I give Vincent a "what the fuck?" look, but he just shakes his head, focusing on the door.

"I've got movement in the lobby," Dominic says, looking at his phone.

"How many?" Vincent asks.

"Eight men total," he answers.

"Eight?" I echo.

Dominic nods. "Must have beefed up security since Augustus was found."

I know there are four of us and we have the element of surprise on our side, but eight guys won't be a walk in the park. I pull out a gun, checking to make sure the safety is off as we wait. Less than a few minutes go by before the sound of the keycard unlocking the door fills the empty silence of the room.

Closing my eyes, I listen for the footsteps. One set, two, three and four. Five, six, seven and... We all wait with bated breath as that eighth set steps inside, then there's the solid thunk of the door shutting before a locking whirr comes from it—Dominic's device in action.

Then all of us move together, taking aim and shooting the first person we can. Each of us land a single target, and four bodies hit the ground. However, four more bodies now have weapons drawn and are firing back at us. Bullets fly, but the noise is surprisingly soft. They too must have silencers on their guns, making this a much more discreet gunfight than I anticipated.

Vincent practically rolls across the floor, emptying a clip into one man's chest while Zayden and Dominic take out opposing men instantaneously. When I pop up from the couch, a hot, searing pain rips into my shoulder, and I curse under my breath as another identical pain burns into my arm, right beside the first. I fire off several rounds and am able to nail the guy in the gut. He curses, his gun falling to his feet as he slumps to his knees.

Vincent comes over to me, quickly examining me while the Graves brothers grab the last man standing.

"Through and through?" I ask through clenched teeth.

Vincent looks me over before shaking his head. Fucking perfect.

He runs into the bathroom, grabs a towel and brings it back over, applying pressure as I lean against the side of the couch.

"What did you get shot for?" Zayden asks.

"I didn't do it on purpose," I scoff.

"With that reaction time, you kinda did," he says before smiling down at the man he's straddling. "Hello, Andre. It's been far too long, my *friend.*"

The way he says *friend* is sharp, eerie. A guaranteed indication that they're anything but. The man groans as Zayden puts more weight on the spot where I shot him.

"Zayden," he grunts. "How are the wife and kids?" He smiles, an evil smile that has Zayden's disappearing in an instant.

"Griggs, grab my bag. I have a sweet treat for this fucking piece of shit," he says.

Vincent walks over to Zayden's bag and rifles through it before his brows furrow.

"C'mon, Griggs, before this fucker bleeds out."

He sighs and walks over to Zayden, handing him two large...

"Candy canes?" Dominic asks.

Not just candy canes, though. Sharpened candy canes. Sharpened to the point of a knife at the end.

Zayden grips one of the candy canes in his hand, then drives it into Andre's left eye. He screams and squeals as Vincent and Dominic both help hold him down. Zayden grabs the other candy knife, because that's basically what it is, before jamming it into his right eye.

Andre writhes and screams, the candy canes moving from side to side like he's trying to wiggle them out of his eyes. The sight of it honestly turns my stomach, or maybe that's the pain from my two gunshot wounds.

"What'd you say, fucker? I can't hear you. Were you saying you laid eyes on my wife and kids?" Zayden snarls before turning and yanking both of the candy canes out, taking Andre's eyeballs with them.

Blood pours from Andre's eye sockets as Zayden tosses the candy-cane-impaled eyes to the side. One of the candies shatters, leaving only a short, jagged piece in the wide brown eye that's currently staring at me. What the fuck?

The next second, Zayden pulls a knife out of his pocket and jams it into the guy's throat. He makes a gargling sound for a few more moments before the noises stop. Casually, like it was any other day, the three of them stand, gathering their things before coming to me.

"You good?" Dominic asks.

I wince as I push myself to stand. "Never been better."

Dominic grips my shoulder, forcing me to bite into my lower lip.

"You're bleeding pretty good. We need to get you patched up. Do we have any contacts in London, Zay?"

He shakes his head.

"We do," Vincent says as he looks to me.

I shake my head. No way are we bringing this shitstorm to Skyla's aunt. No doubt she would help us, but she has two young kids. She doesn't need this shit.

"I'm fine," I grunt. "Call a doctor, pay him off. Whatever."

Vincent purses his lips, then nods before pulling out his phone and typing rapidly on it. I look around at the bloody-as-fuck mess we've left behind and am about to ask what we're going to do about it when Zayden pulls out a can of spray paint and begins spraying a symbol on the wall.

"What is that?" I ask.

He looks over his shoulder at me. "Local gang. They're known for being very territorial. Figured they could take the rap with the feds."

"How nice of you," I say and laugh, cringing as I do. Fuck, this hurts like a bitch.

He shrugs. "I do what I can."

Chapter Twenty Two
Asher

"Yeah?" I answer.

"Wesley was shot," Vincent says coolly, jumping straight to it.

"What?"

"Two shots. A doctor is taking care of him now. He'll be fine after some R&R."

"You could have led with that," I scoff, shaking my head.

The worst-case scenario immediately flashed into my head. Images of having to explain to my wife and uncle that the man they love is gone. Explaining to our children that one of their daddies is...

"We'll be taking a later flight once we get him all patched up. He's fucking staying home next time."

I laugh at that. "Are you the one that shot him?"

"No," he scoffs. "Look after my siren, Putnam."

"Always do," I say, then hang up the phone.

Even though it's been years, Griggs and I have never really warmed to one another. Maybe it's because he's a cold psycho and I really can't fucking stand him. Yeah, that must be it. Somehow, we make it work, though. He loves my wife just as much as I do, and so we tolerate one another, for her.

My phone rings a-fucking-gain. I swear to fuck I'm ready to chuck the thing out into the woods.

"What?" I snap.

"Sorry to bother you. I just wanted to apprise you of a situation," Dane Lewis says.

He's an Elder, a title he inherited from his father, who's long gone. He's also my least favorite. Maybe it's because he's always talking shit. If anyone would be plotting to overthrow me, it would definitely be him and Stroughton. Or maybe it's because when Skyla and I were first engaged, he set his sights on her. Planned to attack her, to violate her. Thank God Griggs got to him before me because I tell you, I wouldn't have just taken his ability to walk.

"What situation?" I grumble.

"There was an incident at my firm. An employee was caught funneling money into a private offshore account. The matter has been... handled, and the cleaning staff are on their way," he says cryptically, though not cryptically enough. If our phones have been tapped by anyone, they'll know exactly what he's saying because he's about as subtle as a brick fucking house.

"How much did he steal?" I ask.

A pause hangs over the line before he speaks.

"Twenty-five million."

I let out a dry laugh and shake my head. Motherfucker. Some little weasel stole twenty-five million dollars of my fucking money? Technically, Lewis runs a finance firm, the biggest and the best, but it's all Brethren money. It was Brethren money that got it on its feet over a hundred years ago, and it was Brethren money that kept the doors open during all the recessions since, so it is by default my fucking money.

"You get my money back by Christmas or Griggs will be taking your fucking arms next," I snarl before hanging up the phone.

There's a knock on the bay window from the backyard, and I look to see Skyla smiling, head to toe in snow gear as she waves. I can't help but smile—just a small one, just for her. Well, that is until Liam bounces towards her, grinning at me like a fool as he makes kissing faces at the window. I swear to God, he's still a teenager. I'm not sure he'll ever grow up. Then again, maybe that's not a terrible thing. This world, this life, it ages you. Faster than you'd like, faster than you want to admit. Maybe having Liam around can slow time down, even just a bit.

I watch as Jackson lines up a snowball and don't bother to warn Liam before it plows him in the back of the head.

Attaboy.

Liam's mouth drops open in outrage. "There's *snow* way you just did that, my dude," he says, and Jackson cackles at the horrible dad joke.

Liam tears after him when he screams and takes off running, and Brooks reaches for Skyla. He's so tiny he basically looks like a blue snowsuit-covered marshmallow. She lifts him easily, resting him on her hip and getting him to wave at me. I smile and wave back as my eyes move to Seraphina, who's currently doing snow angels, while Ryder and Aries build a fort with Ronan's assistance.

I know that I should head back into my office. I have a million and one things to handle that haven't been getting done since we've been up here. Even more so since I don't know when we'll be able to return home to Salem. The Graves brothers assured me this morning that they would be eliminating the rest of the Four Horsemen by Christmas if they had it their way. With it being December 21st, though, I can't deny I have my doubts. We all may be stuck here for longer than any of us desire. I won't be rushing us home without making absolutely sure that all threats have been eliminated.

I called in a team to keep eyes on our home back in Salem. I don't know why—I just had this nagging feeling that it needed to be watched. That if someone was going to come for us, they'd do it when our guard was lowered, when we were at our most vulnerable. It's no different than Wesley calling in the private security firm to watch the cabin without my consent. I swear to God, the man thinks he's one step ahead of everyone when he's nothing but two steps behind. I don't just have eyes in Salem or even Massachusetts, and if he believes that, then he has no faith in me whatsoever.

It's fine, though. I've already vetted the company and the men currently patrolling. All check out, at least enough for my preferences. If they can be hidden and not heard, more power to them. A little backup never hurt anyone.

"Ash!" Skyla says, grinning as she steps in the front door. "You were supposed to come outside, not stand in here sulking and all moody," she teases as she moves towards me.

I give her a flat smile as I pull her towards me, then press a kiss to her forehead. "Sorry, princess. A lot on my mind."

She smiles up at me, but it quickly fades. "Is everything okay?"

Wesley pops into my head. I know Skyla will want to know, but there's nothing to tell. He's being fixed up, he'll be okay, and they'll be home soon enough. There's no sense in worrying her. At least, that's the excuse I give myself because the entire situation is out of my control at this point.

"Yeah, usual shit. It's fine."

She nods and smiles as the door opens once more. This time it's Liam bounding through the house like a puppy hopped up on... fuck, I don't know, puppy crack? Something.

"What are you two doing in here?" he asks, smirking. "Ooooh are we gonna slip in a quickie?" he asks as he begins undoing his pants.

"Liam! All the kids are outside," Skyla admonishes.

"Yeah, outside. And we are inside." He winks as he continues undoing his pants.

"Ronan is out there watching five kids. I don't like those numbers," I say with a shake of my head.

Liam pouts, jerkily redressing himself like a petulant child. "Fine, but promise we can have extra sexy fun time later."

Skyla laughs. "What exactly is extra sexy fun time?" she asks.

He shrugs. "Could be anything. You could suck me off while Ash fucks you. Or Ash could fuck me while I eat you. Ooooh or we can fuck your pussy together, our cocks rubbing against each other until we blow our loads," he says, sinking his teeth into his lip like that's the best idea he's had all day.

Skyla scrunches up her nose and shakes her head. "Don't call it that—blowing your load. Yeah, I don't like that," she says as she heads for the door.

"Fuck! Sorry, I forgot. Until we fill you up so well that you're leaking!"

"No," she says as she steps through the door.

"Fill you with our baby gravy?" he calls out.

The door slams shut and it's quiet for a moment before I give him a flat look.

"Baby gravy? What the fuck is wrong with you?"

He shrugs. "Hey, you're the one that loves me," he says, then he places a quick kiss on my cheek and bounds out of the house once more.

That I do, for some unknown reason.

Chapter Twenty Three
Skyla

I hit the call button, only to be sent to voicemail for the third time. Frowning, I look down at my phone to verify that I have service. Maybe it's something with his phone? Maybe they're in the air. That doesn't make sense, though. They have Wi-Fi on the plane. He could at least shoot me a message.

Wesley promised me he would be home by lunchtime today, and with bedtime quickly approaching, my anxiety is rising. My hands go to my belly, nervously rubbing it as I attempt to calm myself down. Asher told me not to worry, that they'll be here soon. When I pressed for more details like if they were okay, he shrugged it off.

Something is wrong. I can feel it in my gut.

"Hey, I just got off the phone with Zay. They just landed," Blake says as she steps into the room.

"Is Wesley with them? Is he okay?" I ask, unable to mask the fear in my words.

I hear heavy footsteps echo through the hall and look to see Ronan step into the light, though he doesn't look as anxious as I do.

Blake gives me a sympathetic look that has my stomach flipping and my eyes widening.

"Oh my God," I gasp.

"No! No, no, no," she quickly says. "He's okay; he's fine. He was shot, and the doctor said that he needed surgery, but they couldn't go to a hospital. They needed to come back to the States, so the doctor did the surgery in the air."

"At that elevation? In a non-sterile environment? You're fucking kidding me?" Ronan balks, shaking his head.

I look up at him with concern. "Did you know he was shot?"

He looks down at me and nods once. "Ash told me, but Vincent told him that he was fine. I didn't know it was bad enough to require surgery. I..." He trails off, shaking his head as his arm comes to me, pulling me towards him like I'm a security blanket.

"Where is he now?" I ask Blake.

"They were moving him into the car. I guess the doctor recommended anesthesia, but since that wasn't possible on the plane, they loaded him up with as many drugs as he could."

I bury my head into Ronan's chest, imagining the worst. His hand comes to the back of my head, rubbing it soothingly as he speaks to Blake.

"He's gonna be okay, though?"

I turn my head to see her nod. "Yeah, it was two shots. One through his shoulder and one through his arm. They just went down and dirty. Dug in, scraped out the bullets and did what they could to clean up the tissue before sewing him up."

Ronan's body stiffens, but he continues rubbing my head. I think he's the one who needs to be soothed right now, though.

Blake takes the moment to quietly slip away, and I pull my head back to look at Ronan. His features are hard and filled with emotion, no matter how hard he tries to hide it.

"Hey, Ronan. Look at me," I practically beg.

Slowly, he does, the fear plain as day in his eyes now that he's looking at me.

"He's okay."

"He's okay," he repeats.

"We're not gonna lose him."

He closes his eyes for a moment and nods. We stand there in silence for a few seconds before I speak.

"Have you told him yet?"

His eyes open, and he tilts his head. "Told him?"

"How you feel about him?" I say gently.

Ronan has denied having feelings further than lust or friendship for years. We've all allowed it because denial seemed to be where he was content living, and Wesley didn't seem to mind... too much. I can see the shift between them more than ever, though. I see Wesley desperate for his love, for his words. I think he needs to hear them just as bad as Ronan needs to speak them.

Ronan doesn't respond for a moment—then he jerkily nods. That takes me by surprise, but I try not to let it show.

"When did this happen?"

"A few days ago. We were going to tell you, but things have just been so..."

"Insane," I fill in.

He nods. "To say the least. I'm sorry."

I tilt my head to the side in question. "What on earth are you sorry for?"

"I don't know, I feel like I've... cheated on you or something. I love you more than anything in the world—you've been my number one since I first saw you in my pool."

I smile at the reminder as he continues.

"But I... I love Wesley too. How fucked is that?"

I do my best not to invalidate his feelings, but how silly can this man be?

"Ro, you know that I love you; I love all of you. If I can love all five of you equally and it not be cheating, why can't you love Wesley and me just the same?"

He frowns like he doesn't see it that way.

I lift my hand to cup his cheek, pulling his gaze from the floor and back onto me. "It's not cheating. You're in love; you're following your heart. Our relationship is all about trust and communication. I trust you with everything I am. Now, if you told me you and Wesley were running away together and leaving me, that would be a different conversation."

"Never," he insists, shaking his head fiercely.

"Or if you told me you fell in love with another woman—"

"Don't even finish that sentence, baby," he scoffs.

I smile at him. "Then I'm good. *We're* good, and I'm so happy for both of you."

He nods, and though he doesn't say much, I see almost a lightness settle over him. As if a weight has physically been lifted from his shoulders. He stands a little straighter and smiles a little wider.

"I love you—so much," he says.

"I love you more."

I'm gently woken up with the feeling of someone rubbing my arm. My eyes flutter open, and I look up to see Wesley standing over me, wavering slightly as he looks down at me with a smile.

"I'm sorry, little one. Vincent took my phone; I just saw all your messages and calls."

I lean up, and Liam slumps off me, turning around to snuggle with Asher as Ronan's eyes flutter open on my right, looking up at Wesley.

"Hey," he rasps.

Wesley smiles down at him. "Hey."

"I heard you got shot, dumbass," Ronan says, and Wesley laughs.

"I'm only laughing because I'm loaded up with drugs right now. As soon as they wear off, I'm fucked."

Ronan nods at that as he sits up more. "Are you heading to bed?"

"Yeah, just wanted to say I'm sorry for worrying you," he says to me before his eyes come to Ronan. "Both of you."

I smile as Ronan slips out of the bed and stands beside Wesley.

"Come on—I'll help you get settled."

Wesley smiles at him again, then shoots me a quick wink before Ronan slips a hand into his and guides him quietly out of the room. I watch them go with a content sigh before settling back into the pillows, but I'm only alone for moments before Vincent appears.

"Siren," he says.

"I missed you."

He nods as he peels off his leather jacket and begins kicking off his boots and jeans.

"I missed you so fucking much," he says as he climbs into bed with me, wrapping his arms and legs around me simultaneously.

The familiar scent of him fills my senses, and a calming sensation falls over me.

"I'm mad at you, though," I murmur into his chest.

It's like I can feel him frown or, more likely, can just imagine it as he speaks.

"What for?"

Pulling back far enough to look at him in the darkened room, I shake my head. "You took Wesley's phone? So you knew I was calling and texting, worried sick. You couldn't have answered? Shot me a text."

His lips remain mashed together for several moments before he speaks. "I didn't want to give you the wrong information."

I frown, unsure what he means.

"He lost a lot of blood. He had to be carried to and from the plane. The doctor we brought with us only had so much in stock to give him. We thought he was decently fine at first, but... it got a little touch and go."

Fear twists inside me. That's not how anyone else made it sound at all. Maybe that's why Vincent didn't answer, though. He can't lie to me—he refuses. He'd rather go off the grid for a week after he's selected my birthday present, fearful I'll get it out of him because he's *that* loyal.

"You could have told me *something*," I argue.

He gives me a dubious look as his hand softly runs up and down my spine. "Do you honestly believe you would have been content with an 'I've got him. Talk soon' text?"

"Well, no—"

"Exactly. I did what was best for you, siren. You and our baby."

I want to argue, but Vincent decides that our conversation is over and presses his lips to mine. He holds me like that for several seconds, like he craves my touch more than the actual kiss before his tongue slips out, tangling with my own. We sit there for countless minutes, maybe even hours, holding each other, kissing and touching. I try no less than three times to climb on top of him, but each time he gently places me back down onto the bed and resumes kissing me.

I'll settle for now, but I better get no less than three orgasms when I wake up. You know, for pain and suffering and whatnot.

Chapter Twenty Four
Dominic

I know my wife is pregnant. I've known for a few weeks now. What I'm surprised by is that Zayden hasn't figured it out. Her period is his favorite time of the month, and according to the tracker on my phone, it should have started almost three weeks ago. I don't know how he hasn't put two and two together yet. Then again, we have been literally running for our lives and killing anyone we can get our hands on just to keep our family safe.

I understand why Blake hasn't told us yet. If she tells us, then it's real, and I'm not sure she's ready for it to be real. She needs time, she needs to think, and if she decides she doesn't want to go through with it... it'll be really fucking hard to rein in Zayden, but I'll do it, for her. I want a big family and many more babies to come, of course, but I want my wife more. I want her happy; I want her healthy. I want her to be okay, and after she had the boys, she was not okay.

It was the only time in our lives that Zayden and I felt truly helpless. Zay was ready to tie her to the bed for fear that she would hurt herself when we weren't looking. The place she was in was so dark even we couldn't find her. We've never been ones who couldn't tolerate the pitch-blackness this world has to offer, but Blake... she's been through so much already, and then to go through that. I really thought we were going to lose her. So if the sacrifice is no more kids in exchange for a happy, healthy Blake, it's one we can easily bear.

I know that the others don't share as much with their wife as we do with ours, but even Skyla knows that something big is happening tomorrow. It's the day before Christmas Eve, and as much as we don't want to leave, we know we have no choice.

We've tracked the last two Horsemen, Desmond and his brother, Dennis, to the same house—Desmond's winter home in the Rocky Mountains. They're rarely together, so we may never get a chance like this again, and we have to take it before they counterattack.

So, despite the teary eyes of all the kids, we have to leave. The plane is ready and waiting, and we have a plan, a damn good one if I can give any credit to Griggs. It's low risk to us, effective and clean.

"Can I talk to you two? Before you go?" Blake says as she looks between Zayden and I.

We both nod and slowly follow her up the stairs. She steps into the bedroom, then shuts the door behind us and locks it. We wait for her to speak, but instead, she just stares at the door in front of her, like she's building up the courage for something.

When she turns to face us, her strong façade has fallen, and fear has stolen over her features.

"I'm scared," she admits.

"Of what, angel?" Zayden asks, his head titled to one side.

"Of this day, this night. What if one of you doesn't come back? What if both of you don't? I've never been scared of that before, but seeing Skyla's fear with Wesley being shot—it reminded me that you two aren't superhuman, you can get hurt, you do get hurt and... I'm so scared," she says, a tear dripping down her cheek.

Zayden is the first to rush to her, cupping both of her cheeks as he kisses away her tears. "You have nothing to fear. This will be the easiest mission we've executed in so long. We won't even be within firing range."

"How?" she asks with a frown.

"Griggs found old inspections that suspected a natural gas leak in the house they're staying in. All we need to do is widen that leak a bit, let off some spark and—"

"Boom," Zayden interrupts me.

"Sounds like you'll be within shooting range. You have to break into the fucking house."

Zayden rolls his eyes like it's child's play, which for us, it is.

"Angel, it's going to be fine. *We* are going to be fine."

"Promise me," she says as her eyes come to me. "Both of you promise me that everything will be fine, that you'll both come back to me in one piece. Promise me everything and more will be okay."

Zayden shares an uneasy glance with me. We don't often promise things, if ever. There's always the slight risk of disappointment, and if for some reason we broke our promise, we'd never be able to forgive ourselves. It's a risk we'll have to take, though, because she needs this from us.

"We promise," we both echo.

She nods shakily, blowing out a breath before she looks to Zayden and presses her lips to his. He practically jumps at the chance, his hands moving everywhere before he's lifting her into his arms, carrying her to the bed. I watch them for a few moments as clothes are shed and moans start filling the space.

My cock hardens, and I reach inside my pants, pulling it out, then dragging my hand up and down its length. Fuck, I love seeing her this way. I've always had a thing for voyeurism, but with Blake... sometimes I enjoy watching her get off more than actually having sex with her. It's exciting, it feels forbidden, and I come so fucking hard every time.

I work my cock in a steady rhythm as I watch Blake slowly sit on Zayden. They both let out pleasure-filled groans as she begins grinding on him, then she beckons me with a crook of her finger. I go because how could I not? How could I not go anywhere this goddess asked? I'd kneel before her from sunup to sundown if she so wished it.

I stand at the edge of the bed, and she reaches for me, but I stand just out of reach, shaking my head. She huffs in frustration, but excitement flares in her eyes. She enjoys putting on a show for me just as much as I love seeing it.

"Please, Dom. Please," she begs.

Something in her tone has me wavering, abandoning my voyeurism in this moment. The need in her voice is visceral, and I crawl onto the bed beside her.

"Where do you want me, babygirl?"

"Inside me, together," she moans as she continues riding Zayden's cock.

I reach for the side drawer and pull out a bottle of lube. I rub it against her asshole, then push a finger inside first.

She groans. "Yessss."

After a little more lube, I push another in, allowing her to set the pace as I stretch her.

"Dom, please just fuck my ass," she whimpers.

My cock literally leaks pre-cum at her words, and then I'm covering myself with lube before pushing the tip against her hole. Slowly, I push inside her, and she squirms and squeals as I continue inch by inch until I'm fully seated in her ass.

Her breaths come in gasps as she attempts to compose herself before she picks up her rhythm once more.

"You promised you'd come back to me, you promised," she says as she takes us both.

Zayden thrusts in as I thrust out, before I push in and he pulls out. It's a balance we've perfected over the years, optimal pleasure for all involved as her babbled words blend together.

"We know, angel, and we intend to keep that promise," Zayden says through clenched teeth.

"Always," I groan.

She nods, grabbing one of Zayden's hands and resting it against her belly before taking one of mine and doing the same. Her eyes move to ours in turn, back and forth as she speaks.

"Come back to me; come back to us."

Her words linger in the air for a moment before her orgasm takes over. I feel Zayden follow her, and with her contracting muscles, I'm a goner right alongside them. We all moan and grunt out our releases before slumping together. Not a word is spoken for minutes; all that can be heard is our labored breathing and the muffled sounds of goodbyes from downstairs.

"Angel?" Zayden asks finally.

"Yeah?" she pants.

"Are we really having another baby?"

The air is quiet for a moment before Blake stirs, slowly pushing up to look at both of us.

"We're having another baby."

My hand grips her hip, holding her tightly, and I press a kiss to the back of her neck as both of Zayden's hands come to her belly, holding it reverently as he looks to her.

"I promise, I'll never let the darkness take you again."

"Neither of us will."

She swallows roughly, nodding as she looks between us. "Whatever happens, we'll face it... together."

We all nod in agreement at that, and she lets out a laugh that sounds almost like a cry.

"We're having another baby," she says, smiling as if the thought is just now hitting her.

We're having another baby.

Chapter Twenty Five
Zayden

I know I need to focus, but I can't stop bouncing my knee. My excitement is practically radiating out of me. I'm gonna be a daddy again. We're having more babies. There's no doubt in my mind that she'll have multiples again, and I wonder how many she'll have this time. I hope it's a whole fucking litter.

"Calm the fuck down," Dom grouches from the driver's seat.

I turn to look at him. "What's crawled up your ass?"

"Nothing. I'm just as excited as you are, but I've known for a while, so I'm not buzzing in my seat. We have a job; you need to focus. We're going to take out the last remaining Horsemen. This has to be flawless, Zay."

I roll my eyes and look out the window, pulling out my knife and flicking it open and closed mindlessly. I know it has to be flawless. In any other situation, I'd be a little uneasy. I mean, we're going up against Dennis and Desmond Volkov. If it were any other day and we were planning a hand-to-hand fight, my adrenaline would be buzzing. It almost doesn't even feel fair this way, though.

We've already studied the blueprints of the house and found that there's a small cellar door on the northeast corner. A quick pick of the lock, I slip in, cut the gas lines, then leave this handy-dandy twenty-pound C4 brick Dom linked to an app on my phone and... boom.

Honestly, I don't even know why they came with. I could do a job like this solo in my sleep. Maybe it makes them feel important.

As we approach the private drive, my excitement over my angel's pregnancy becomes the sole focus in my mind once more. There wasn't time to ask questions like how far along she is or how she's been feeling. All things I'll have addressed as soon as we're out of here. As soon as we're done, we can go home. We can all settle in back in Seattle and resume our life pre-Beatrice Volkov's death.

Again, I get it. My bad.

Dom parks the car a few hundred yards away from the beginning of their driveway before turning the engine off. Together, we slip on our skeleton masks before turning to see Griggs pull a black hoodie over his head.

I laugh. "We'll need to get an honorary one made for you, Griggsy."

He pins me with an unimpressed look before flipping me off. I smirk as I look to Dom, who's readying a gun in one hand and the brick of C4 in the other. He passes the brick to me and nods.

I nod back before we all open our doors as one. Our feet crunch against the frozen ground, one step at a time, and we never let our eyes stay in one place for too long. Our heads move like they're on a swivel as we each assess our surroundings. Good thing we do too, otherwise we might not have spotted the two guards standing just inside the gated wall surrounding the property.

I reach up the brick wall and feel a slightly protruding brick that will do the job. Clutching the edge, I lift myself up as high as I can before grabbing another and another. I'm almost to the top when I see Griggs already up there, waiting for me. Show-off.

Looking down, I see Dom is right beneath me, so I perch myself on the edge of the wall as Griggs does the same. Together, we wait for the two guards to walk beneath us before we leap. I land on top of the guy to the right at the same moment Vincent does the man on the left. A startled gasp escapes my target as we fall into a roll on the ground. I quickly wrap him up, holding his body in place with my legs as I reach for my knife. A few quick jabs to the neck and his struggling gasps are silenced. When I check how Griggs is doing, I see his target has a knife embedded in one eye and his neck is broken into an unnatural angle.

I raise my hand to him for a high five. Griggs stares at me incredulously for a moment before obliging with the lamest high five I've ever seen.

Dom lands beside us with a soft thud then before fully rising to his feet. He grabs one of the bodies and tosses it over his shoulder before gesturing to the other one. "Grab him. We'll toss them in the basement before we blow the place."

Griggs nods and lifts the limp body over his shoulder before we begin walking. The buzz from the kill has already started vibrating from the tips of my toes to my fingers. Combine this excitement with the giddiness of my angel being pregnant and I feel as if I'm about to burst. I wish I could channel this energy the way I crave, but I know this job isn't one to get up close and personal on. The Volkov brothers are too much of an even match for us, and we need to come back home to our wife and kids.

We sneak across the back lawn as Dom hands me his phone with the surveillance cameras pulled up. I flick through each screen until I find them. The pieces of shit are sitting around a fire, drinking a bottle of something like it's their goddamn job. I watch as Desmond claps Dennis's shoulder, forcing him to stumble, then they both seem to break out into laughter.

Pieces of fucking shit.

They sit here and get drunk, laughing like a couple of hyenas while holding a hit out on my family. Sending people after my children, my wife, my brother. We've killed their two closest friends and their sister, and yet they laugh it up without a care in the world. As if they're untouchable, unreachable.

I move to the cellar door, pull out my tools and quickly begin picking the lock. It takes hardly any effort at all before it gives way. I push the door open all the way, gun drawn in anticipation for company. If they were smart, they'd have had *some* backup inside at least.

I crawl into the cellar and head for the gas lines while Dom and Griggs dump the bodies on the floor. After hopping up onto an old steel box, I go to cut the lines—then freeze.

"Dom," I say.

He comes over to see what I see. Steel-enforced casing, even around the wiring. I could bust out an electric saw, but the risk of the spark catching the free-flowing gas and blowing us to hell along with the Volkov's is strong.

I look over my shoulder to see him shake his head as Griggs speaks.

"Just place the bomb on top of the gas main. That's all you can do at this point."

Dom shakes his head. "There's no guarantee it'll catch. We need these fuckers charred."

Vincent shrugs. "It's the best option we have."

He's right, and as much as I hate to leave things messy, we don't have a choice. I place the brick on top of the gas main, then the three of us turn to head out of the house, but a figure appears in the doorway. He's staring at his phone and seems just as surprised to see us as we are to see him. What the fuck? Where did this guy come from?

He drops his phone in an instant, pulling out his gun to shoot Griggs. I sweep my foot across the ground, dropping the kid before I pull a knife from my side and send it through the air. It embeds itself in his throat, and his eyes widen in shock as a gargling noise escapes him. In the same instant, a bullet from Dom's gun burrows right between his eyes, dropping him to the floor. I look to my left to see Dom unscrewing the silencer attached to his gun before looking at Griggs, who's still on the floor.

"Have a nice trip?" I ask.

He doesn't say anything as he pushes to his feet. I pull him up the last foot until he's balanced.

"Goddamn, kid, with how many times I've saved your life, we're going to have to start up an account or something."

"Who said I couldn't have handled that guy on my own before you tripped me?" he scoffs.

"Whose knife killed the fucker?" I counter.

"Not yours. Your brother's bullet did the job," Griggs says back.

"Are we seriously still standing here talking? We need to get the fuck out of here!" Dom snarls like we're the unreasonable ones here.

He leads the way, and Griggs and I quickly follow him out of the house. We make it across the lawn without being spotted and are up and over the gate before anyone can attempt to confront us— or more likely shoot us dead.

Dom starts the car, and we drive away just far enough to keep the house within viewing distance before I look down at the app Dom installed.

"See you in hell, fuckers."

With a click of a button, a deafening boom rings out through the entire goddamn city. I swear, people one state over heard that shit. One more second passes before a secondary boom comes, and the house is engulfed in flames. There goes the gas main.

Flames rage, swallowing up the expansive mansion, licking at the perfectly manicured lawn and gardens around it, leaving nothing but ash and destruction in its wake. We all stare at the uncontrolled beauty of it, relishing in the satisfaction of a job done. The pleasure of knowing that the Four Horsemen have fallen, once and for all, is a greater feeling than I could put into words. The world is a better place, a safer place. Hell, if we signed our names on this act, I have no doubt we'd earn ourselves the Nobel Peace Prize. Or at least we should.

Sirens sound in the distance, and Dom takes that as his cue to put the car in drive. We head in the opposite direction as I tune the radio to the police scanner we've set up.

"Unit 224 inbound. Fire en route behind me. Oh... oh my God," the gargled voice exclaims. "We need backup. As many rigs as we can get. The fire is moving to the neighboring properties!"

Whoops.

We stay tapped into the scanner until we begin to lose connection. That's when Dom pulls over and we wait for those words we need. We all sit silently as hours tick by. The fire seems to be truly unmanageable, but finally at 2:13 AM, those blissful words hit all our ears.

"Several casualties... Fucking burned to a crisp."

Burned to a crisp.

Music to my fucking ears.

Chapter Twenty Six
Vincent

The place went up in a blaze. Four bodies were extracted and were so charred, the causes of death couldn't even be verified, meaning the fucker with the cracked neck in the cellar will be seen as just another casualty of the fire.

Of course, I'm sure they'll be able to figure out that the fucking chunk of C4 left behind was used to start the fire, but the trail will go cold, the file will be sealed and that will be the end of it. After all, there isn't exactly a line of people demanding justice for the ruthless mercenaries that have been terrorizing Europe and North America for the last two decades.

"Hey, I've been looking for you," Skyla says as she comes around the corner.

I push away from the desk, closing the laptop—and the news article on the mysterious fire—as I turn to my wife, spreading my legs as I gesture for her to come closer. She comes to me willingly, like our pull is inevitable. Or maybe that's just how I view it to be.

Skyla climbs into my lap, nuzzling my neck as she speaks against my skin. "The kids were asking for you—they want to open presents."

"It's Christmas Eve," I counter. "They shouldn't be opening any presents until tomorrow."

She pulls back far enough to roll her eyes at me before laughing. "You and I both know those kids are so spoiled, it would take them five business days to open all of their presents. They need to get a head start."

I smirk at that. The guys did go overboard this year, as did I, though I can't say it's different than any other year or birthday. There's no way they won't grow up to be spoiled rotten, at least in some ways. Not when they have five dads willing to hand them the world at any given moment.

"Blake and the kids are going home tomorrow; her husbands too of course," Skyla says.

I nod, though I don't miss the hint of sadness that touches her words.

"Isn't that a good thing?"

She shrugs. "I was kinda getting used to the company. It's not like I don't have other mom friends, but Maggie and Bridgette are usually busy and... I don't know."

Nodding, my thumbs rub gentle circles against her lower back. "You made a friend and now she's leaving to go back to her life on the other side of the country."

She pouts. "It sounds childish when you explain it like that."

"I don't mean it to. I'm sorry them leaving upsets you, siren. It is for the best, though. The Graves family brings trouble... as you've witnessed first-hand. It's best for all that they go back where they came from."

Skyla turns her head curiously. "I thought you liked them, or at least Zayden."

I let out a dry laugh. "I'm not sure even his wife likes him. He's Zayden Graves. He's... Zayden."

She watches me closely, like she's waiting for me to elaborate, but really, that's all I have to say on the matter. Shaking my head, I attempt to pacify her, to ease the sense of loneliness she's suddenly feeling.

"It's been... an experience to work beside someone so well known, so formidable."

Honestly, that was the nicest thing I could have said about him, so I think that's more than good enough.

Skyla rolls her eyes as if she knows that's all she'll get out of me before moving on to a new topic. She reaches over to the floor and grabs a wrapped present I didn't notice her bring inside. The wrapping paper is a deep crimson with a crisp white bow and a little peppermint name tag dangling off it with my name on it.

"Merry Christmas, Vincent."

I take the package from her, looking deep into her hypnotic eyes in thanks before tearing open the wrapping. The paper gives way easily, revealing a white clothing box. When I lift the top, I find a black sweater inside. The material is soft like butter as I rub it between my fingers. It's not my style at all, if you could even say that I have style. I definitely don't wear collared sweaters, though.

Still, she bought it for me and went through the effort of wrapping it for me, so of course I'm going to appreciate it.

"Thank you, siren. I love it."

She smirks. "You're such a liar. I didn't know what to get you, but I did think you would like the smell."

My brows furrow as I lift the sweater to my nose and inhale gently. A familiar smell hits my senses. It's dulled, for sure, having been wrapped up for an unknown amount of time, but the smell is instantly recognizable.

"Siren, why does the sweater smell like your cunt?"

She giggles mischievously, a smile playing at her lips as she wiggles herself in my lap. "Do you like it?"

"You know I love it, but I want to know how your smell got all over this sweater."

Skyla pushes to stand, then slowly strips off piece after piece of clothing. My eyes waver from her body only for a moment to check that the door is already locked. Perfect.

"Hmmm, you know. I'm trying to remember, but it's slipping my mind. Maybe if you gave me some incentive, it might jog my memory?"

I lift an unimpressed eyebrow as my gaze eats up her naked flesh. Her body only grows more attractive with each day of pregnancy. I swear to fuck, growing a human has never looked so goddamn delectable.

"Incentive?" I ask, allowing each syllable to roll off my tongue as I stand.

She smiles like she has all the power in this situation, and most days, she does. But in the bedroom, or whatever room we deem appropriate, she will always be my submissive.

Before she can react, I'm bending down, peeling her leggings and panties off before tossing them to the side. She goes to ask what I think I'm doing but doesn't get the chance to finish her question before I'm lifting her up into the air and pressing her back against the wall. She gasps in surprise as I lift her higher, wrapping her legs around my shoulders so I can bury my face in her cunt.

"Vincent! Shit, put me down! You're gonna drop me." She squirms as she holds her belly protectively.

I pull back, looking up at her with her taste practically dripping off my chin as I swear to her, "I would never or could never let you down, in any facet of the word, siren. When you're in my arms, know that you are the safest you could ever be. You both are."

She softens at my words before one of her hands comes to the back of my head, fingers wrapping around my hair as she shoves me back between her thighs. I go willingly, my tongue licking through her like I've never been gifted such a thing in my life. That's because with her, every time feels like the first time. I'm not ignorant to my mortality, to how quickly life can be snatched away. After all, I'm usually the one doing the snatching. I will forever treasure every moment I share with my wife and my children. Even if I vow to lay my life down for theirs, nothing is ever guaranteed, and that thought right there is what keeps me up the most at night.

I feel my siren about to fall apart on my tongue, but I deny her, pulling away abruptly and leaving her whimpering in my arms. Her eyes are closed, her mouth is open, and disappointment is spreading across her features.

"Wha... what's wrong?" she asks.

"Tell me how the smell of you got all over my 'present'?"

Her playful smile returns, and she shakes her head.

Carefully, I lower her to the ground before guiding her over to the desk. After wiping it clear with one hand, I lift her to the edge before lining my cock up to her. She squirms and moans as I run my tip through her, never actually sliding inside, though.

"Vincent," she groans in frustration.

"Tell me," I say, swirling my tip across her clit.

Her eyes fall closed, and her head tilts back before I'm smacking her clit with my cock. Those perfect green eyes fly open, landing on me as I speak once again.

"Tell me, siren. Now."

"Wesley and I fucked in the dressing room when we were buying your present at the mall. He cleaned me with it."

I scowl at her words. "So it's not just you on the sweater, it's him too?"

I can tell she's attempting to hold back a laugh, but I'm not in the laughing mood. Maybe the others would get off on the fact, but for me, it's a reminder that I don't own my wife in all the ways I crave. That in order to have her, I have to share her. The idea has become easier to live with the longer we're together, but I'll never overwhelmingly accept it. She knows it, and so do they, and I don't appreciate the goddamn reminder when I'm trying to make love to her.

I smack her clit with my cock again, and again I look down at the tattoo I got for her. It's been years, but I'll never tire of seeing her name permanently embedded into my flesh.

She gasps at the smack before I do it again and again.

"Vincent," she moans.

"No," I gnash. "I shouldn't fuck you. I should leave you here to squirm and suffer."

She frowns at that as I shake my head before pushing my cock inside her. Another needy gasp escapes her as I sink deeper, resting my head into the crook of her neck as I speak against her delicate skin.

"Of course, you know I've never been able to deny you a single thing, siren."

I begin moving my hips, pushing in and out of her as she attempts to meet my thrusts.

"I want a new sweater, with only your smell on it. I want you to walk into a store, purchase a sweater, come home and use it to get yourself off."

"Would it help if I told you this sweater was mainly used to rub my clit?" She smirks like she thinks she's funny before another moan ripples through her.

"No," I answer flatly.

Her smile comes to me, her eyes desperate and wanting. "Whatever you want, Vincent. It's yours."

That's more like it.

I move my hand to her clit and rub quick circles over it with my thumb that have her falling apart within seconds. Her pussy constricts around me, and it's all I need to follow her over the edge. My cock jerks as I empty myself inside her, making sure to fuck every drop deeper. I can't get her more pregnant than she already is, but it doesn't hurt to try.

When our movements pause, I pull back, looking down at my perfect siren as she smiles up at me with a satiated smirk.

"Merry Christmas Eve, Vincent."

I lean down and press my lips to hers, my words ghosting just above her mouth as I speak.

"Merry Christmas, siren."

Chapter Twenty Seven
Seraphina

A loud noise wakes me up. I blink a few times before rubbing my eyes. My room is too dark, and I can't see nothing.

I tuck myself under my blankets more and whisper to the twins. "Did you guys hear that?"

"Hear what?" Aries asks as Ryder keeps on snoring.

He snores a lot. Every night since they've been here, after our parents put us to bed, they sneak in here to sleep on the floor. Then they wake up early and sneak back into their room. Sometimes I don't even hear them go. It sounds silly, but I like them in here.

At first they started sleeping in here because we didn't want to stop playing a game even though it was bedtime. Then they just started coming in because. I put all the stuffies on my bed on the floor for them so it would be a fluffy sleep.

We heard the grown-ups say that tomorrow they're going home. I'm glad that I'll get to see them open the Christmas presents I made them. They haven't been here long, but they've become some of my bestest friends. Thinking about them moving far away makes me so sad. But Aries promised they would come see me lots, and I believe him. I believe them both.

I wait for the sound again, but it's quiet. Maybe I was just dreaming. Then it happens again! A loud thunk from outside. This time it sounds different. Maybe closer... Maybe it's...

"It's Santa!" I say as I hang over the bed.

"You think?" Aries asks before smacking Ryder's arm. "Wake up! Santa is here."

"What?" Ryder asks. "Santa?"

"C'mon!" I say as I jump out of bed.

I hear Ryder and Aries following as we run into the hallway. I look to the living room, standing on my tippy-toes to see over the railing. The Christmas tree doesn't have any new presents, and the stockings are still empty. Sadness fills me before another thunk comes from the backyard.

"He's here!" I say, jumping up and down before running down the stairs.

"This is a bad idea," Ryder says.

"Stop being such a baby," Aries says with an attitude.

"I am not a baby!" Ryder retorts as I head for the door.

I almost make it too before Ryder puts out an arm, stopping me before grabbing my coat from the closet and putting it on me.

"It's too cold out there," he says as he concentrates really hard on zipping up the jacket, then he forces me to step into my snow boots as they do the same.

I smile at him, but I can't help but bounce on my toes. If we don't hurry, we might miss him.

Aries opens the door, and together we all run out to the backyard. I look around in every direction, high and low. I look for his sleigh or his reindeer, but I can't find them. I hear that sound coming from the back of the house again, though, so I take off sprinting, leaving the boys in the dust because if anyone is going to catch Santa, it's going to be me. After all, I'm the one who woke up to him first.

My cheeks hurt as the snow falls around us, but I can't stop smiling. I'm going to finally catch Santa on Christmas Eve. I'm going to—

Chapter Twenty Eight
Zayden

A piercing scream wakes me up. I'm on my feet and out the bedroom door in less than two seconds, grabbing the knife on my bedside table as I go. In the hallway, I run into a disheveled-looking Griggs, who appears to be in a similar fight-or-flight state.

"What the fuck was that?" Ronan asks, stepping out of his room as my angel emerges from ours.

"Vincent? What's going on?" Skyla asks as a few of her other guys pile out of the room.

Liam pokes his head into a room a few doors down. His body goes rigid, and he runs to my boys' room.

"The kids are gone!"

"WHAT?" I snarl as another ear-piercing scream rings from outside, followed by the sound of my boys shouting.

Chills cover my body, and I'm leaping down the stairs, taking the entire flight in three steps before tearing through the living room. I barely stop to slip on shoes, then my feet are ripping through the frozen ground.

The snow is falling fast, practically blinding me, but it's not enough to stop me seeing what's in front of me. A man in a long black trench coat is standing just under the glow of the back porch light, a crowbar at his feet and little Seraphina wrapped up in one of his arms, held by her throat with a gun to her head.

My gaze flies around us to see Ryder holding his stomach, groaning, and Aries unconscious on the ground, a gash above his eyebrow. A rage without end fills me as I move closer to the figure, freezing in place as his eyes meet mine.

No.

There's no way.

No fucking way.

Desmond motherfucking Volkov.

How? How did this motherfucker survive? The house blew the fuck up and took out two neighboring properties alongside it. I'd recognize him anywhere, though. And now that I'm able to focus on him, I can see the extent of his injuries. He looks like hell. His face is half charred, the flesh raw and red. It's as if he hasn't yet sought medical care, instead letting vengeance fuel him. Based on the look of his flesh, from his bare, burnt hands to his singed skull, I'd say an infection will get him in less than twenty-four hours. If only I wasn't about to gut him like a goddamn pig.

Twirling the knife in my hand, I speak calmly and coolly as my eyes move to my boys once more. My steps are calm and even, though I feel nothing of the sort.

"Volkov, I must say, I've seen you look better."

An evil grin—at least I think it's a grin; it's hard to tell with half his face burned off—is visible in the glow of the house lights.

"I must say, I'd have to agree, Graves."

"It was stupid of you to come here. You realize that, yeah?" I ask as I inch my way closer and closer to the boys, keeping my eyes trained on Desmond's gun.

I hear several footsteps crunching in the snow behind me, and I know that my brother's behind me at least, with at least three more people closing in. But if I can hear them, then so can—

"That's close enough! Anyone takes one more step and I'll blow her goddamn brains out!" Desmond snarls.

I pause, and the others do the same. I'm about thirty yards from him. Definitely close enough to sink this knife into his neck but not close enough that my knife will land faster than he can pull the trigger.

"Daddy, help her. Please," Ryder begs.

Christ.

Desmond seems to get a kick out of my son begging. He smirks at him before turning to me. "Oh yeah, Daddy, please. Please come save the little brat. No doubt she'll grow up to be a whore just like her mommy. Five husbands? I'm sorry you weren't raised with a better role model, sweetheart," he says to Seraphina as a soft cry escapes her.

I don't attempt to talk him down; I don't ask him to let her or my boys go. The more weakness I show, the more I plead, the worse the situation becomes for all. When you're in a moment between life and death, you maintain focus and reason. You strike first, always, and if you don't have the upper hand, you fake it until you do.

"How'd your brother fare?" I ask as I gesture towards his burns.

The sound of a door shutting upstairs in the house has his eyes swinging in that direction, and I take the opportunity to step another five feet or so closer. Any inch I can get will produce a more favorable outcome.

Desmond's smile falls away, anger taking hold of him as he jerks Seraphina roughly, squeezing her throat until she's sputtering. "He's dead. Thanks for asking. You've officially wiped out all my siblings, Graves. I look forward to affording you the same treatment."

"I only have one brother," I bargain.

"Yes, I'm afraid an eye for an eye won't quite do. Your slut of a wife will have to do as penance for my sweet Beatrice," he says, his sister's name like a brokenhearted prayer on his lips.

If he wasn't an unhinged murderous fuck who's been trying to slaughter me and my family, who's now hurt my boys and is holding a little girl hostage, I might feel a sliver of remorse. Killing Beatrice was truly an accident. His brother, not so much, and the death I'm now fantasizing for him... that one definitely won't be an accident.

My eyes move and stop on Dominic, who's just behind Desmond. He's crouched down in the bushes, motioning to Aries, who's now conscious, and Ryder to stay quiet. He'll never get to the boys in time, though, not before one of the three of them is shot. Or Seraphina. Or all of them.

Deciding I need to distract him, I take a step to the side, forcing Desmond to turn to face me, Seraphina still in his grasp, silent tears falling down her face.

"Do you want to know what happened that night? How she died?" I ask.

He doesn't respond, but I can feel his attention on me as I continue walking until his back is completely to my boys. Dominic creeps closer, near silently snatching Aries off the ground and pulling him to safety before trying to get closer to Ryder.

"I was called for a hit on her boyfriend. I didn't know who she was at the time; she was just another girlfriend. You know the deal."

"I know the fucking deal. I called the hit myself, asshole. I specifically said him, not her. HIM!" Desmond snarls.

I nod. "Truly, it was a mistake. I took care of him, but she woke up, found me, tried to plunge a fucking metal comb into my neck. We grappled with it, and it ended up in her chest. I called a medic to the place, but—"

"She was already dead. Yes, I know," he snaps.

I flick my gaze behind him. Dominic has Ryder in his arms now and is disappearing into the darkness once more.

"She said something before she died," I say, piquing his curiosity.

Desmond frowns. "What did she say?"

My mind races with possibilities, outcomes and plan Bs for how to get myself and Seraphina out of this unharmed. We outnumber him clearly, but a bullet moves faster than a blade, and I don't know what kind of shot, if any, anyone else has.

"This is all my brother's fault."

Desmond's face contorts in shock for a moment, like he doesn't fully process my words. Once he does, though, rage fills him.

A shadow moves behind him, and I'd recognize that slinky movement anywhere. He's too far, though, so I make my move.

I raise my hand, gripping the cool metal of the knife's handle before sending it sailing through the air. It spins beautifully, cutting through the heavy snow before sinking into his shoulder. But before the blade enters his skin, a loud pop sounds, and a sharp burning slices into me.

Looking down, I see a hole in my thigh before blood begins pouring out of it. Fuck. That shit hurts.

I look up to see Desmond point the gun at my head once more, a stolen breath escaping me as one of my boys calls out, "Close your eyes! It's a scary part!"

Seraphina slams her eyes closed as Griggs draws up behind Desmond, gripping his jaw in one hand as he draws a blade across his neck. A spurt of crimson blood splatters the pure white snow before Desmond's body collapses.

Vincent squats down beside the gargling body and turns his head to the side.

"Merry fucking Christmas."

Epilogue
Blake

I've experienced a lot of traumatic events in my life. I've had more "scariest nights of my life" than any one person should. I will tell you, though, I'm not sure much will top running outside to see my children hurt on the ground, then one of my husbands shot, only to be narrowly saved by a fellow mercenary.

Yeah, you know what, I completely realize that our life is way more fucked up than I give credit for.

As the guys all ran outside to follow Zayden, they instructed Liam to stay back and "protect the girls and the young ones." I actually feel bad for punching Liam in the face. Skyla told me not to, though, because she was about to do the same. When he was disoriented, we took off outside. How could we not have when we knew our babies were in trouble?

The gasp of horror Skyla let out when she saw her little girl held hostage with a gun to her head was something I felt all the way into my gut. It was followed up by seeing my own boys hurt, a wave of pain and panic only a parent could truly know.

Dominic scooped the boys up seamlessly, dragging them to safety, but that still left Seraphina in harm's way. Despite Wesley set up on the lower roof with a sniper pointed at Desmond Volkov's head, no one moved a muscle. Not even when Desmond shot Zayden; not when he lined up for a kill shot.

The instant Vincent cut Volkov's throat, Skyla and I took off for our babies. We couldn't be stopped, and no one even attempted to do so. Seraphina kept her eyes closed the whole time, sobbing hysterically even as Skyla wrapped her arms around her, shushing her gently. Still, though, she didn't open her eyes until Aries and Ryder came running over, both insisting that it was safe.

I asked Ryder what he meant about Seraphina closing her eyes for the scary part, and he explained to me that they'd started watching horror movies with Liam when everyone else wasn't around, something that absolved my guilt of punching him rather quickly. Seraphina apparently tried to be brave but would get too scared at certain parts, so one of the boys would tell her when to close her eyes for a scary scene, and when she could open them again.

It's still amazing to me how quickly the kids bonded. It's been a little over a week, but it may as well have been a lifetime that they've all known each other. Seraphina made each of them friendship bracelets with their names spelled out in beads for Christmas, and Ryder drew her a picture of herself while Aries carved a heart out of a chunk of wood. Don't ask me where he got the knife or how he learned to carve wood, though it doesn't take too many guesses to figure it out.

Despite the... eventful Christmas Eve we all had, we were able to get the kids to sleep while some of the guys took care of Zayden's bullet wound. They even had a whole IV set up at the ready with extra bags of O-. At least we aren't the only fucked-up family with insane day-to-day lives.

The little ones had no idea what happened, and we tried to keep it that way. The excitement of Christmas had definitely turned somber, but I think the gratitude of us all being alive and together helped repair that.

A feeling of relief I hadn't known I needed washed over me as I lay in bed with my boys, all four of them, the next night. I refused to let the twins go back to their own room, insistent on watching them all night. Same with my husbands.

Now it's the next day, though, and our bags are packed, and our car is ready. We're heading home to Seattle, just as planned, only one day behind. We're all more than ready to be home, and yet a bitterness follows our departure. I can't stop crying, and though I'm chalking up ninety-five percent of it to hormones, I know a piece of me will miss them all.

The boys are going back and forth hugging Seraphina, pulling her out of each other's arms one after another, and it breaks my heart. They promise to come visit soon, and Seraphina says the same. I have no doubt that if we don't plan something ourselves, we'll wake up in the middle of the night to their beds empty and a car gone. Six years old or not, they're their fathers' sons.

"Blake," Skyla says with a watery smile.

I give her one in return as she pulls me in for a hug.

"Promise you'll call me anytime. I want to hear all about how this little one is treating you," she says.

"Of course, and don't you dare give birth without letting me know. We'll send gifts or something!"

She waves me off like that's unnecessary before pulling back.

"Thank you, Skyla. Thank you all for... everything."

Vincent comes up beside her, wrapping his arm around her waist as he nods. He's the quiet type and absolutely not a hugger, but I hope he hears my sincerity. Without his help, without them all, I'm not confident my entire family would still be standing here today. I know he was repaying a debt to Zayden, but in my opinion, he did so and then some, and now I'm the one eternally grateful.

"Appreciate the assistance, Griggsy. Maybe next time you

could move in before the fucker shoots me, though?" Zayden says, clapping Vincent on the shoulder.

"Griggsy? Oh hell, forget Vinny. That is absolutely your new nickname," Liam cackles.

Vincent lets out an annoyed grunt before shooting daggers with his eyes at Zayden. "Thanks for that."

"I do what I can." My husband grins like an asshole.

I smack the back of his head.

"Ow! What was that for?" Zayden balks like he's shocked I would lay a hand on him.

"Your sons are watching—show them how we properly thank someone for saving our lives."

Zayden gives me a deadpan look that I return with zero hesitation. Dom comes to stand on the other side of me as the others mill about in the background.

"Your favor is more than repaid," Zayden says. "If any of you ever need anything... we're a phone call away."

"We'd offer the same, but I'm not sure I enjoyed my family taking your phone call," Asher snarks.

Dom lets out a short scoff before offering his hand to Asher. He shakes both Dom's and Zayden's hands before looking to me.

"You all will always have a place to stay in Salem."

A smile touches my face. I like the sound of that, though I'm sure they're just empty words. But the illusion of keeping in touch fills something inside me.

A few more heartfelt goodbyes—and inappropriate remarks by both Liam and Zayden—later, and we're in the car, heading to the airport, where Asher's private jet is waiting to take us back home. We board the massive plane mostly in silence. Well, the guys and I board in silence. The twins are bouncing off the fucking walls and have broken three things before we've even taken off.

Sighing, I shake my head as I look out the window.

"What's on your mind, babygirl?" Dom asks as he comes to sit next to me, wrapping his arm around my shoulder.

I look up at him. "Everything... nothing."

He nods like he gets it. He always does.

He leans down and presses his lips to mine, lingering for so long, I think he's never going to stop. At least, that's my hope.

Something jostles us, and I look to see Zayden kicking Dom's foot before taking the seat across from me.

"Quit fucking hogging my wife," he says.

Dom doesn't even give him the time of day before turning to face me. "I was thinking, it would be nice to come see this side of the country when it's not completely frozen."

"Yeah?" I ask, not able to mask my hopeful tone.

He nods. "I was thinking maybe late summer? Fall even?"

"You have to keep in mind, I'll probably be ready to pop by then," I say as I rest my hand on my belly.

Honestly, for a moment even I forgot about the new addition to our family.

Dom nods thoughtfully at that before brushing a piece of hair out of my face.

"The house I'm looking at has more than enough bedrooms—and is just down the road from some very willing and helpful hands."

I pull back to look at him fully, silently asking him to clarify.

"A house?" Zayden asks. "We moving?"

Dom looks to him and shrugs. "If that's what our wife wants. Or maybe it could be a vacation house. Just a thought."

"You guys would be willing to do that?" I ask, looking between the two of them.

Zayden rolls his eyes, leaning forward to rest his elbows on his knees. "Angel, when are you going to get it through your beautiful, perfect head? Whatever you want in this world, in this life, it's yours."

I smile softly as Dom nods his agreement.
"Salem in the fall sounds absolutely perfect."

Thank You

What do you think? Should we end it there? Close these stories once and for all and move on? Yeah, I don't think so either. Many more times are coming, so many evil fuckers to kill, so many holes to fill, so little time, or however that goes.

If you haven't read the Gallows Hill trilogy or Graves... well, this book was probably a little more than confusing for you! If you have and are searching for your next book, I've got you covered!

Gallows Hill Series—a dark academia reverse harem
Damnation (Prequel)
Deceit
Descent
Demise

Standalones
Graves—an MFM stalker romance
Deliverance—an FF secret society romance (spin-off from Gallows Hill)
Gratify—a forbidden age gap
Jagged Harts—an MMA enemies to lovers

The ONS Series—interconnected forbidden romances
One Night Seduction
One Night Scandal - Coming Soon
One Night Surrender - Coming Soon

The Alphaletes Series—interconnected football romances
The Loyalties We Break
The Walls We Break
The Hearts We Break
The Rules We Break

Reviews mean everything to indie authors, so if you could take a moment to leave a review, I would be so thankful!

Review on Amazon & Goodreads
Find me on Instagram, TikTok, Facebook, and my Facebook Reader Group

Make sure you are subscribed to my newsletter and following me on socials to stay up to date on any upcoming releases, special announcements, and giveaways!

Acknowledgments

To my alpha, Sara, I'm so grateful for you! We've talked about this story idea for so long, and now that it's finally here, I'm so happy I had you by my side through it! Though I definitely tore my hair out at times, your support meant the world to me and truly helped shape this book!

To my betas, Courtney, Kelly and Rachel, thank you so much! Your attention to detail and input really helped elevate this book in ways I could have only hoped! Thank you for your opinions, encouragement and overall amazing commentary (especially regarding the head puppeteering). Thank you all for your hard work, patience and just being flat-out amazing.

To my editor and proofreader, you two are out here doing the Lord's work. Without you two, I can't even begin to imagine what kind of nonsense this book would be published with. Thank you for the expertise, insight and overall talent that you brought to this project!

To my street team and ARC readers, thank you all for your support! Every page read, every review left, and every post made truly means the world. I'm not even a little shy to admit that I have hands down the best people behind me.

To my readers, whether this is your first book by me or you've been by my side since day one, thank you. There are millions of authors out there, billions of books and you chose mine. Each one of you pushes me to write when my fingers ache, plot when my brain is mush and keep moving forward when I'm ready to give up. You are all the best readers anyone could ask for, and I love each one of you desperately.